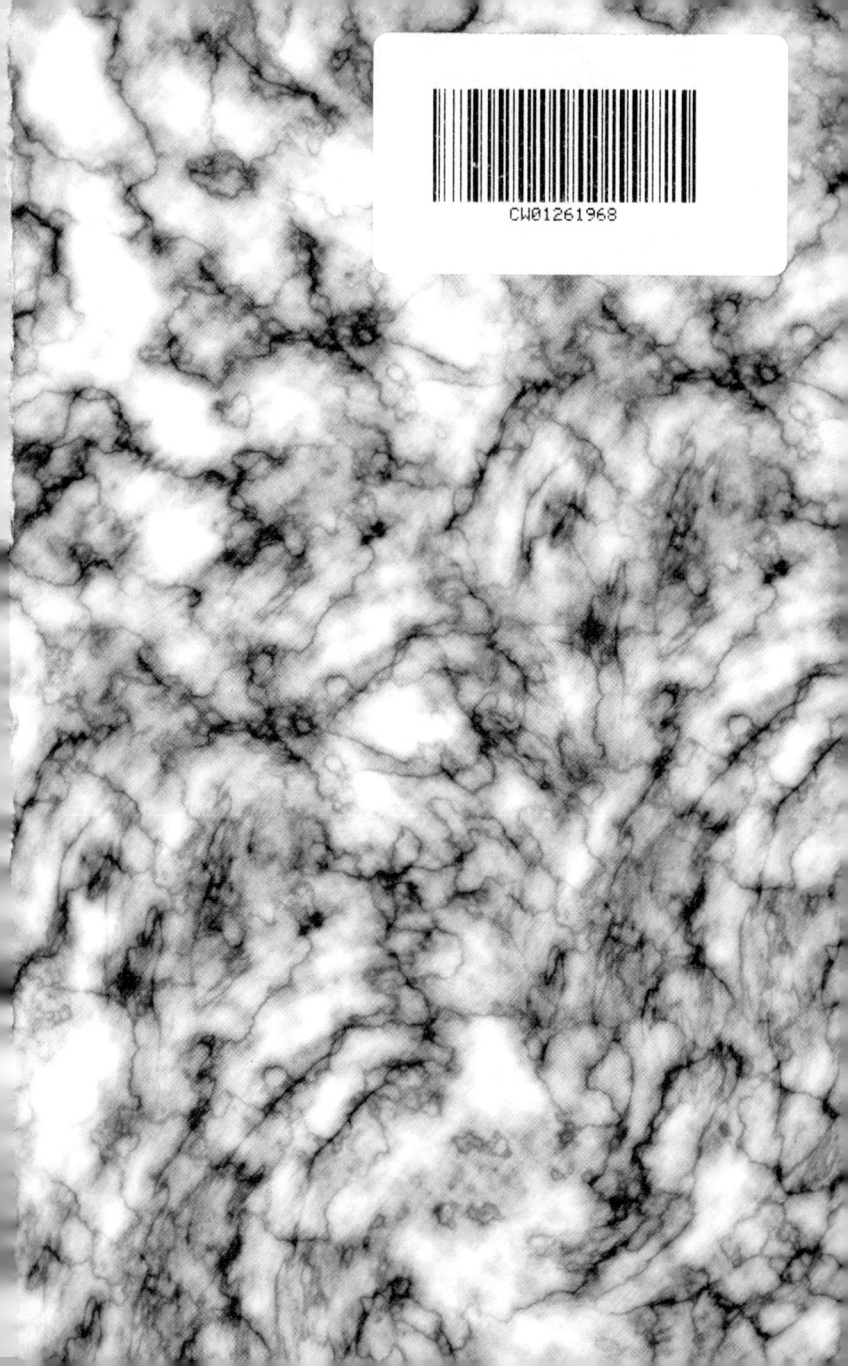

Praise for BODY ELECTRIC

"The complications of a father-daughter relationship; the vicissitudes of a society eroded by the glare of reality TV; a concrete vision of life and death as it radiates out from the men and women who work in the Nashville morgue. BODY ELECTRIC is a sophisticated, complex portrait of human relationships — and a novella, that most difficult of forms, that encompasses a real, whole world."
ERICA WAGNER

"BODY ELECTRIC is as thoughtful, controlled and unsentimental as its coroner protagonist. A terrific novella."
NED BEAUMAN

"BODY ELECTRIC is an exquisitely executed story. C. E. Smith maps out the intricacies of the human heart through death and heart break with an abundance of compassion and the type of wisdom that reminds us why we read fiction in the first place."
DINAW MENGESTU

BODY ELECTRIC is the winner of the 2013 Paris Literary Prize, an international novella competition for unpublished writers, organized by Shakespeare and Company, and The de Groot Foundation. In 2013, the prize was judged by Erica Wagner, author and literary editor of THE TIMES; Rebecca Carter, literary agent with Janklow & Nesbit; Sylvia Whitman, owner of Shakespeare and Company; Ned Beauman, author of BOXER, BEETLE and THE TELEPORTATION ACCIDENT; and Dinaw Mengestu, author of THE BEAUTIFUL THINGS THAT HEAVEN BEARS and HOW TO READ THE AIR. The two runners-up of the 2013 Paris Literary Prize are SORRY FOR PARTYING by Tessa Brown and DAM DUCHESS by Svetlana Lavochkina.

Born in Atlanta, Georgia, C. E. Smith studied literature at Stanford and medicine at Vanderbilt. His short stories have appeared in THE BEST OF THE BELLEVUE LITERARY REVIEW and elsewhere. He lives with his wife and children in Louisville, Kentucky, where he works as a radiologist.

THE WHITE REVIEW

THE WHITE REVIEW
243 KNIGHTSBRIDGE,
LONDON SW7 1DN

SHAKESPEARE AND COMPANY
37 RUE DE LA BÛCHERIE
75005 PARIS, FRANCE

FIRST PUBLISHED 2013 BY SHAKESPEARE AND COMPANY PARIS
AND THE WHITE REVIEW

BODY ELECTRIC © 2013 BY C. E. SMITH

THE RIGHT OF PERSON SO LISTED TO BE IDENTIFIED AS THE AUTHOR
OF THIS WORK HAS BEEN ASSERTED BY THEM IN ACCORDANCE WITH
THE COPYRIGHT, DESIGNS AND PATENTS ACT OF 1988

ISBN 978-0-9568001-8-3

DESIGNED BY RAY O'MEARA
TYPESET IN JOYOUS (BLANCHE)
PRINTED AND BOUND BY MEMMINGER MEDIENCENTRUM AG, GERMANY

ALL RIGHTS RESERVED. NO REPRODUCTION, COPY OR TRANSMISSION, IN WHOLE
OR IN PART, MAY BE MADE WITHOUT WRITTEN PERMISSION OF THE PUBLISHER.

THEWHITEREVIEW.ORG
PARISLITERARYPRIZE.ORG
SHAKESPEAREANDCOMPANY.COM

BODY ELECTRIC

C. E. SMITH

I

2

TABER HATES TO BRING HOME THE SCENT of death, especially the night of his daughter's first date, her homecoming dance. After he showers and puts on fresh clothes, he still detects a residue of mephitic rot, but at this point the smell exists only in his mind, like the afterimage that follows a flash of light. In his early days as a forensic pathologist, he would come home convinced he reeked of death, that he was somehow contaminating the sheets and towels and dishes. He'd worry about it even after his wife (a strange kind of intimacy, one person sniffing the skin of another) insisted she couldn't smell anything.

He stands outside his daughter's bedroom door and says, "Katie, it's almost seven."

"I need a minute," she snaps—her voice surprisingly close, just beyond the door.

He goes downstairs and microwaves a wedge of leftover pizza and eats while standing at the counter. He takes a beer into the living room and sits in front of the television. If the doorbell rings before she's ready, he must prepare himself for the daunting task of conversing with an unfamiliar teenager, a wrestler named Ken McGavin. Taber has vague worries about his motives. A plain, slightly overweight 17-year-old girl, unaccustomed to romantic attention of any kind, might be expected to welcome even the crudest advances.

On TV a muscular fireman searches for his soulmate among the bikini-clad sirens sharing his jacuzzi. One of the women, in a separate interview, insists that she's usually not the sort to fall in love after only a week. An amazing thing about reality TV, that blatant contradiction of terms, is the apparent conviction of its participants that what they are saying is noteworthy.

But it isn't for fear of looking foolish that he objects to *American Autopsy*, the reality show set to begin filming this very week at the morgue where he works. Nor is it his aversion to the title, what with its false implication of a uniquely American method of post-mortem examination. What bothers him about *AMERICAN AUTOPSY*, besides the inevitable conflict between the reality of his work and its entertainment value, is that the patients being filmed, the cadavers, are incapable of giving their consent.

None of his partners share his intuition that it's a bad idea to film an autopsy. Where the Chief Medical Examiner, Brandt Michaelson, sees opportunities for publicity and recognition, Taber sees a potential lawsuit, a violation of the public trust. He's considered an official complaint to the state medical board, but that would accomplish little beyond killing his friendship with Michaelson.

He picks up the remote and turns to the news. A mile-long chain of bras hangs from telephone poles in downtown Nashville. Each bra supposedly commemorates a local victim of breast cancer. He turns off the TV.

At ten after seven it occurs to him that his daughter's date might be waiting in the driveway, so he goes to the front door and gazes out the window. The streetlights shine even though it isn't quite dark. Across the street a row of Diane Adler's upstairs windows suddenly illuminates and he catches a glimpse of her husband, sweaty from a workout, pulling off his shirt. A cat bolts across the Adlers' yard.

He turns at the sound of his daughter's heels on the hardwood stairs. He tries to remember the last time he saw her in a dress.

"Don't look at me like that," she says. "You're making me nervous." Accustomed to flat-soled sandals, she clutches the railing to keep from tottering on her high heels.

"You look beautiful," he tells her.

"I guarantee you," she says, touching the gold strand that encircles her neck, "that everyone who sees me, except for you, thinks I'm ugly."

This is probably true. It seems she was made in his very image, with little to no consideration for gender. But it's amazing what a difference her efforts have made, along with the ministrations of Diane Adler. He isn't used to seeing her in make-up—it almost conceals the acne covering her cheeks and forehead. The ruffles flaring out above her knees have the effect of reducing the apparent girth of her hips.

As she walks into the living room, her hand runs along the edge of the wainscoting, and there is audible friction between her nylon-encased legs. They sit down and he regards her shoes, brocaded with floral designs. It was Diane Adler's idea to blacken the worn down toes with an indelible marker.

She slouches with her legs casually spread, the velvet ruffles between her thighs impeding what would otherwise be a view of her crotch.

Tentatively he asks, "Shouldn't you cross your legs when wearing a dress?"

Her nature is rebellious, and he expects her to spread her legs even wider, ridiculing his outdated ideas of feminine posture, but with a gesture of annoyed acquiescence she throws one leg over the other. She folds her hands in her lap. Her shoe dangles from her toe. Through her stockings, he can see a mole near her ankle and he worries it might have malignant potential. He can also make out the scar on her knee where many years ago a neighborhood boy struck her with a shovel.

"Don't you have something to do?" Katie asks. "It's so weird how you just sit there looking at me." She has arranged her hair in a bun, with long needles holding it in place.

"I thought I'd keep you company while you wait for Ken."

"Where is the remote?" she asks and before he can answer she finds it on a stack of magazines.

5

She flips to the show *BACKTALK WITH BARBARA BROWN*, and they are intrigued to see the host, known to her fans as Babs, wearing a fluorescent green cast on her forearm. She brandishes it like some kind of cudgel and says she broke her arm fending off an assailant. The man would have raped her if not for the canister of pepper spray on her key chain. A representative from the pepper spray company demonstrates various products, one of which launches a toxic stream powerful enough to knock an apple off a golf tee from ten feet away. Another device, conveniently worn like a bracelet, is triggered by a simple flick of the wrist.

"He better hurry," Katie says when her date is almost thirty minutes overdue. "All I need for my dwindling self-esteem is for some wrestler to stand me up for the Homecoming Dance."

She nods toward the television. "Maybe they'll test the pepper spray on that rapist."

Text at the bottom of the screen explains that Barbara Brown's guest is a convicted rapist who wants to be castrated at the expense of the state. The guest doesn't look like a rapist. He has a pudgy face and a lopsided bow tie, and he gazes about with wide-eyed innocence. He says he has a close relationship with his mother.

"There's a surprise," says Taber.

The rapist tells the audience about his collection of vintage science fiction posters. He portrays himself as a man-child enslaved by his own testicles, a victim.

"A victim of being stupid," Katie says.

The talk-show unveils a surprise guest: the rapist's mother. They embrace and she takes a seat beside him, patting his knee. She expresses support for the state-funded castration of her son. It was her idea in the first place, and if she had the money she would gladly pay for it herself. She blames his undoing on internet pornography.

She keeps glancing at her phone, no doubt hoping for a text from

Ken.

"Isn't it kind of cool to show up late?" he asks.

"I hate it when you say that word."

Barbara Brown consults a urologist, who appears by video rather than in person. He offers to castrate the rapist, or anyone for that matter, for just two thousand dollars.

If Taber would cooperate with *AMERICAN AUTOPSY*, he might find himself in this urologist's position, an expert in a tie and starched white coat, lecturing Barbara Brown's audience on some fine point of toxicology.

The house phone rings and Katie frowns at the Caller ID. She motions to throw the receiver to her father, but he gets up and crosses to where she sits on the couch.

"Did you get pictures?" Diane Adler asks, a note of warning in her voice.

"He's not here yet," Taber says, offering his daughter a half-smile.

"That little son of a bitch," Diane Adler says, and then louder, "That little bastard."

"Leave his mother out of this," he says, trying for humor, but Diane is already relaying the news to her husband. Katie seems transfixed by the television. He strolls into the kitchen, listening while Diane and her husband argue. She seems angry with him for not being angry enough.

"I think he's just a little late," Taber says.

"A little?" she says. "The pimply asshole found something better to do and stood her up." He imagines her staring furiously at her husband as she speaks, longing for a reason to blame him for all of Katie's social hardships. "I'll kill him," she says.

He laughs. "If Katie doesn't get to him first."

"You're so stiff," she says. He doesn't know if she's talking to him or her husband. He opens the refrigerator and finds a single can of beer behind a week-old plate of spaghetti.

"Should I come over?" she says in a whisper.

"I think she'd be embarrassed," he says, opening his beer.

When Taber returns to the living room, the paroled rapist is trying to avert his eyes but keeps sneaking looks at a voluptuous model dancing in a bikini and high heels. His mother holds his hand and tells him to be strong. She looks at the audience and says, "Can't you see him suffering?" By now her son's eyes have locked onto the writhing bikini. He removes his hand from his mother's. She looks at Barbara Brown with an expression of resignation and utter helplessness. And then, to the horrified delight of the live audience, he lunges for the dancer, only to be restrained by stage-hands. The rapist's mother screams, "Don't hurt him!" She grabs a stage-hand by the hair and falls ridiculously onto Barbara Brown's coffee table. Over the closing credits, Barbara Brown reveals the theme of tomorrow's show: "Husbands Who Rape".

Katie puts on her shoes and says, "I just remembered something. When I made plans with Ken, we decided to meet at school."

She rises, settling her crimson ruffles, and plods across the rug.

"I hope you're not late," he says, almost embarrassed by the transparency of her lie.

She opens the closet and finds her black overcoat. "Oh, they won't mind starting the dance without me."

He watches her through the window. She has to walk on the grass to reach her car, a two-door Honda he purchased when she turned 16. She stumbles when the points of her heels penetrate the sod. Across the street Diane Adler opens her front door to admit her little dog Michelangelo. She waves—either at Taber or Katie, perhaps both of them—as the dog scurries inside, its upright tail brushing the hem of her dress. A misshapen pumpkin sits under the porch light with rudimentary eyes and a smiling mouth. She calls out and Katie responds with a wave before dropping into her car.

The Honda flares its brake-lights and spurts exhaust. He watches for a moment, deliberating, then jogs across the lawn. "Wait!" he calls, increasing his pace. His daughter opens the door, because the mechanism for rolling down the window has broken.

"Forget the dance," he says, pretending not to notice her tears.

She stares straight ahead. "I'm late."

He clasps his shoulders against the cold. He sees Diane Adler watching them from her front porch. Their eyes meet and she raises a hand and covers her mouth with the tips of her fingers, as if frightened by what she might say. He makes gestures over the roof of the car urging her back into her house.

"We could watch some more TV," he says.

Katie takes a deep breath and exhales loudly through her nose. She cuts the ignition. They walk toward the house and she places her hand in the crook of his elbow and the pressure fluctuates as she teeters. She goes upstairs to change out of the dress. He waits for a time, and then goes up and knocks on her door. He finds her in bed reading, her head propped on a stack of pillows.

"I don't want to talk about it," she says.

"You have nothing to be ashamed of," he says, sitting on the edge of her bed.

"The guy didn't show up. It was probably some kind of prank, and he and his friends are all laughing about it."

"Little bastards," he says.

She looks at him, and her face hardens into an expression of irritation. He suddenly regrets his patronizing scrutiny. He wishes he had let her drive away—that he'd allowed her to think she'd concealed her rejection, at least from him. Her attention goes back to the book. He slumps where he sits, his arms crossed, and stares at the carpet. When she turns the page he stands up and leaves.

9

❡

The next morning he sits in the kitchen wondering if he should call Ken McGavin's parents. He looks up the number in the University School directory. The parents' names are included: Tina and Brian. He seems to have met them at some point, perhaps at church—Katie mentioned they were members of St. Bernard's. He tries to remember what they look like, but all that comes to mind is a vague impression of bland affluence. For no clear reason, he's beginning to think of them as golfers, owners of foreign cars and large SUV's—the sort of people to foster a reputation for southern gentility. The sort of people to be outraged by their son's reprehensible manners.

Should he make the call? What would he say? He never intended to be an overly involved parent. Of course he wants her to succeed in school, in life, but on her own terms. Next year he'll encourage her to major in a subject she likes, rather than one that will land her a job. He's never complained to teachers or school administrators—not even when she was unjustly cut from the band, or denied an insignificant part in the junior high play because some other girl looked better in a leotard. Katie is learning to work out her problems on her own.

If he called the McGavins, she'd view it as nothing short of humiliation—worse perhaps than what she's already experienced. But he wouldn't necessarily be calling them on her behalf. What if it was some accident that kept the boy from showing up? Perhaps Ken's parents watched him leave in his suit or tuxedo, and now sit waiting for him to return, assuming he spent the night with a friend. For all Taber knows, they might call here any minute: Have you seen our son? He never came home last night. Taber would restrain the inevitable feeling of relief, and afterward chastise himself for caring more about his daughter's self-esteem than the very life of

Ken McGavin.

He bides his time by calling the morgue. There's no answer: no one comes in on Saturday unless there's a body. He checks online to see which of his partners is on call. Karen Landman. He sends her a text: *Any cases?* Half a minute later she replies: Not yet.

He dials the McGavins. He dials without thinking. The more he thinks about it, the longer he'll put it off. While it rings, he tries to convince himself that he's beyond mere anger, that what he wants, first and foremost, is to make sure Ken McGavin is alive and well.

The answering machine: a female voice, presumably Ken's mother Tina. When the beep arrives, he hangs up.

II

12

THE FIRST MORNING of filming, he retreats into his office and studies microscopic slides from last week's autopsies, all the while keeping track of the additional vehicles in the parking lot—two rental cars and a white van. A man in scrubs hurries out to the van, and when he opens the rear doors, Taber makes out tripods of some kind leaning against a stack of metal trunks. The man retrieves a shoulder satchel, but just as he closes the doors, a plastic Coke bottle falls from the van and rolls underneath. He sets down the satchel and kneels behind the van, gripping the bumper. He has to lie on the pavement to reach the bottle.

AMERICAN AUTOPSY isn't Taber's first brush with reality TV. Four years ago he and Katie were walking through Hillsboro Village when they came upon a group of fraternity members engaged in flagrant hazing. The pledge, wearing nothing but a diaper, crawled on the pavement while his cohorts shouted taunts and pelted him with garbage.

Katie put her hands on her hips and said, "Leave him alone!"

This was totally out of character for a 13-year-old girl who was timid at baseline, and even more so in those months after her mother's death from breast cancer. The men looked like linemen on a college football team. If it came to some kind of altercation Taber wouldn't fare any better than his daughter. He took her by the elbow and urged her to keep walking, but she refused to back down.

"This has to stop," she said.

"We have the right to treat our pledge however we want," said one of the fraternity members, surprisingly calm.

"No one's getting hurt," said another.

"We aren't breaking any laws."

The diaper-clad pledge waited on his hands and knees, perfectly still, maintaining an attitude of total submission even as his tormentors turned their attention elsewhere.

"It's a matter of dignity," Katie said.

Dignity: Taber winced at the word. How often had the doctors and nurses spoken of preserving it in his wife? And at what point had it become code for withdrawing care? At the funeral, Father Nick had emphasized how Lizzie had kept her dignity even to the very end. Was Katie thinking of her mother when she used that same word, or when she took off her jacket and laid it across the pledge's back?

The fraternal abuse turned out to be staged for hidden cameras. The show, "Smoking Gun," specialized in what commercials described as "experiments in human nature." In hindsight Taber should have seen through the artifice—the so-called frat boys were too old, the Greek letters on their matching tee-shirts too obvious.

When the film crew emerged from a parked van, Katie began crying so hard she couldn't answer any of the questions put to her by the youthful host.

"Dozens passed without doing anything," the host said into his microphone. "What made you intervene? What went through your mind?"

She sobbed, incapable of anything more than a one-word response. The host, who of course had no way of knowing about her mother, eventually gave up on the interview altogether, simply patting her back and repeating the words "It's all right." When the show aired a few months later, ominous music and baleful close-ups of the frat boys heightened the sense of danger, but Katie's breakdown was presented as little more than a fleeting wave of emotion. Taber of course was glad to see her portrayed as a hero and not some raving hysteric.

¶

In the employee lounge he finds the coffee pot near empty. He pours out the dregs, presses a filter into the bowl, and adds a packet of grounds. While the water boils, he strolls down the hall to the autopsy suite.

From the vestibule he's able to see the cameraman—who half an hour ago was crawling after a Coke bottle in the parking lot. He wears blue surgical scrubs, the shirt untucked, and a bulky pouch cinched around his waist. The derangement of his facemask attests to his inexperience wearing one. Except for the camera on his shoulder, and perhaps the waist pouch, he looks like a medical student on his first day in surgery.

Taber had expected a more elaborate undertaking—wires on the floor, standing lights, scrambling assistants, even a director in a folding chair. Perhaps this will be less obtrusive than he thought.

The cameraman sidesteps around the autopsy table while Michaelson gestures with bloody gloves.

"Every autopsy report contains three categories," Michaelson says as Taber opens the door. "The mechanism of death, cause of death, and manner of death."

Taber recognizes the lilting cadence of Michaelson's TV persona, a mask polished by years delivering sound bites for the local news. Whenever an autopsy draws media attention, it's almost always Michaelson who makes TV appearances, regardless of his involvement in the actual case.

"If I were to have a typical heart attack," Michaelson says, "the mechanism of death would be myocardial infarction, the cause atherosclerotic coronary vascular disease, and the manner would be natural. In our case today, the mechanism was carotid exsanguination, the cause a gunshot wound, and the manner homicide."

Early in his career, Michaelson achieved minor notoriety for his handling of the celebrity autopsies that seem to occur on a regular basis in Nashville. His predecessor so despised publicity that Michaelson, in only his first year out of residency, became the unofficial spokesperson for any cadaver even remotely famous. It wasn't long before local journalists and news stations were calling him whenever a story involved forensic science.

But his appointment as Chief Medical Examiner—a position for which Taber was passed over—likely had as much to do with his social connections as his media presence. He grew up in the posh neighborhood of Belle Meade and married the granddaughter of a senator. He frequents charity balls and country club functions, and though he clearly enjoys these events, he never mentions them to Taber without scoffing at their superficiality, or blaming his wife for his seemingly endless social obligations.

Taber peers down at the body: an African-American male with a bullet wound to the neck. The massive swelling is typical of arterial injury. There are streaks of grey in the man's beard and afro, a military tattoo on the forearm. He has calloused palms, the faint indentation of a long-worn wedding band. In the thigh is a second gunshot wound—or a first, as the case may be—which Andrea, the fellow in forensics, probes with tweezers and a scalpel.

Michaelson says, "This is Martin Taber, one of our top pathologists."

The sudden attention jars Taber—as if till now he'd been lulled into a false sense of privacy, even invisibility, by the camera's lack of interest.

"Hello," he says, thinking his smile must look ridiculous.

His eyes fixed on the camera, he tries to come up with something intelligent to say. He wonders if he needs one of the transmitters Michaelson and Andrea wear on their collars. He takes a step closer to the microphone protruding from the camera. Its fuzzy surface is speckled with bone dust, no doubt from when they sawed off the top of the skull. His distorted reflection in the lens reminds him of the homunculus, or "tiny man," the theoretical figure used by anatomists to map brain function.

It seems Taber was a selling point when Michaelson initially courted the production company. His academic credentials would add an element of scientific legitimacy—or so Michaelson claimed. The producers must have bought into the idea, because his unexpected refusal threatened to sink the entire venture. In fact, it was only after Taber agreed to do interviews and promotional segments that they officially tapped Nashville as their morgue of choice.

He stares at the camera. It seems like everyone, even the cadaver, is waiting for him to speak. A pressing silence, but all that comes to mind is that single word: *homunculus*.

Andrea rescues him from further awkwardness by finding the other bullet—a shapeless chunk of metal in a gravelly slime of bone bits and clotted blood. At Michaelson's prompting she displays it for the camera before dropping it into a plastic bowl.

"Would you mind using metal instead of plastic?" asks the cameraman.

"What do you mean?" Andrea asks.

"When you drop the bullet in the bowl," he says, "we'd prefer you use metal instead of plastic."

"Are you kidding?" Andrea says with barely suppressed laughter. "We can't change procedure on account of sound effects."

She turns to Michaelson but her expression is concealed by the glare in her eye-shield.

"Billy has a point," Michaelson says. He rattles the bullet as if to demonstrate the suboptimal acoustics. "We should have stainless steel emesis basins in storage."

"I don't see how this is relevant to the case," Taber says. He doesn't know what angers him more—the bowl issue, or the fact Michaelson would side against Andrea.

Chaquita, the autopsy diener, presses a button on the wall. A voice crackles over the intercom and she leans close to the speaker and says, "Bring us a small metal bowl please."

While they wait Michaelson turns to Andrea and says, "How well do you know the brain?"

"Well enough, I guess."

Having hardly worked with her in the four months since she began her fellowship, he has yet to appreciate her seemingly unlimited grasp of minutiae, or her tendency, no doubt unintentional, to expose the ignorance of those who try to test her knowledge, particularly in the area of human anatomy.

"Can you name this structure?" Michaelson asks, placing the tip of his probe to one of the inch-thick slices of brain laid out in rows on the counter.

The question is far to easy for Andrea, who could probably name every bulge and groove in *CLINICAL NEUROANATOMY*.

"The rostrum," she says.

"Excellent," Michaelson says, but it's evident from his forced enthusiasm that he doesn't know the precise meaning of *rostrum*—that all he was asking for was the more general *corpus callosum*.

Andrea keeps her back to the camera whenever possible. Her reluctance might be edited to seem like obeisance to Michaelson. No doubt Michaelson and the producers have considered the dramatic value of a pair of physicians in the roles of mentor and understudy. The problem is that there isn't anything he can teach her that she doesn't already know.

Andrea was their only applicant for the fellowship program. Residents generally gravitate to the more lucrative fields like dermatologic or surgical pathology. Taber and Michaelson established the fellowship three years ago, mainly at Taber's initiative, but as of last spring, they had yet to receive even a single application, only the occasional inquiry from foreign medical graduates and residents from marginal programs. Andrea had an offer to do a prestigious derm-path fellowship at the University of Pennsylvania, but changed her mind in June, about a week before her scheduled move to Philadelphia. Taber wonders if she realizes that by applying, even at the last minute, she saved the fellowship program from near certain elimination. The group wouldn't have tolerated the cost and embarrassment (though relatively mild on both counts) of going another year with an empty program.

He catches himself staring and quickly looks away. The last thing he wants is for her to feel like an object of lust among the older men charged with her education. He's been irritated to see both Michaelson and Tamagi all but groping her with their eyes. How could she not have noticed? Perhaps she ascribes prurient motives to all of them, Taber included.

¶

The next day Taber eats his sack lunch in the break room where the muted television displays a church service. When the preacher lifts his Bible for emphasis, the sleeve of his robe slides down and reveals the faded black tattoo of a handcuff encircling his wrist.

At the next table, Giles Tamagi and Karen Landman, husband and wife pathologists, whisper out of Taber's hearing. They use matching non-disposable chopsticks to share some brownish, congealed substance interspersed with cubes of tofu. Taber winces at the odor—it mingles with the lingering putrescence of his last autopsy.

It was a particularly bad case—suitable perhaps for *AMERICAN*

Autopsy had Taber been willing to consider it. The body, a man in his thirties, had been partly eaten by a pet dog. Taber and Andrea had to work fast because of the smell. He didn't bother pointing out the different types of beetle and maggot spilling from a crater in the abdomen. Taber still doesn't know how the man died. Perhaps he'll find the answer when he dissects the brain. He plans to let it soak in formaldehyde for at least a week before trying to cut it.

"People of earth, I come in peace." This has been one of Michaelson's standard greetings since medical school. He wears a spandex biking outfit with TEAM NASHVILLE emblazoned on his chest. The bike itself, which typically hangs from a hook in his office, now waits in the corridor behind him.

Trailing Michaelson is a man whose most striking feature is his size. Massively obese, he has to turn at an angle to fit his midsection through the door.

"Let me introduce Aaron Barnes," says Michaelson, "the producer of *American Autopsy*."

Tamagi and Landman stand and introduce themselves with mumbles and obviously limp handshakes.

Barnes wears jeans and a red tie that deviates over the side of his voluminous abdomen. His jet-black glasses look like they might have been inked onto the pale skin of his doughy face and completely bald scalp.

"And this must be the brilliant Dr. Taber," Barnes says, offering his hand.

"I've told Aaron all about you," Michaelson says.

They hover at his table, seemingly with more in mind than a simple introduction, so he gestures toward the pair of empty seats.

"Have you done anything we might have seen?" Taber asks.

"My partners and I have almost twenty years' experience in television," Barnes says, putting a hand to the back of his head. "Our main focus is reality TV. Are you familiar with *Lust Mansion*?"

"I'm not," Taber says.

In a glance he can tell that Michaelson, while himself having no qualms with *Lust Mansion*, would have preferred to keep it from Taber.

"I'm sure you're aware of the enormous popularity of forensic science," Barnes says. "*American Autopsy* is going to be a huge hit."

"No doubt," Taber says, trying to be polite.

"My goal is to capture the heroism of medical examiners."

Taber almost laughs. "You can't be serious."

"You put maniacs and serial killers behind bars," he says. "You stare down evil and stand for the truth even when it could get you killed."

Staring down evil? Does he think they carry guns as well? Taber turns to Michaelson, who shrugs and looks away. Taber wouldn't be surprised if Michaelson embellished their work in order to bring the show to Nashville. Barnes will be disappointed if he expects serial killers and games of cat and mouse.

"As I'm sure you know," Taber says, "I'm not completely sold on the idea of filming autopsies."

"What is it that bothers you?" Barnes says.

Taber watches for some gesture or conspiratorial glance to pass between Michaelson and Barnes, but Barnes abruptly lurches back in his seat, whipping his hand behind his head as if on the verge of bellowing with laughter. He takes a deep breath, which evolves into a protracted yawn.

"Obviously you're free to make your own decisions," Barnes says, "but I'm just afraid you're missing out on a great opportunity."

"That's a risk I'm willing to take."

"We don't want to interfere with your work," he says. "We're here to observe, nothing more."

"It seems to me an essential part of any autopsy is privacy," Taber says, but lowers his voice at the thought of Tamagi and Landman at the next table. "Whether the patient himself would have wanted his body to be filmed like that."

"We live in an age of absolute transparency," Barnes says.

Absolute transparency. He keeps hearing that phrase. What does it even mean?

"I for one believe that people deserve to know," Michaelson says. "They have an inalienable right to know what could happen to them and their loved ones after they die."

"If people want to know about autopsies—" Taber stops himself before saying he could recommend a few textbooks. He changes tack: "It seems like a camera would threaten this idea of absolute transparency. Who can resist performing, even on a subconscious level?"

"In my experience," Barnes says, "true professionals are so absorbed in their work that they forget the camera altogether."

"I feel like a show like this would create an incentive—if not to lie, then at least to make an autopsy more interesting. A suicide would make for better television than an accident."

Michaelson chuckles courteously, as if to acknowledge an attempted joke, and says, "We'll check the data after a few months of filming, to see if there's a statistically significant difference."

"One thing you should remember," Barnes says, "is that the success of *American Autopsy* depends largely on the credibility of its subjects."

"We see surgery practiced on TV all the time," Michaelson says. "Do the surgeons reinvent themselves on camera? Do they alter their techniques to make their cases more compelling? I seriously doubt it."

"If you think of an autopsy like any other medical procedure,"

Taber says, "would you want your rectal or psych exam aired to the public?"

"Sure," says Barnes, "as long as I've given permission, and as long as my identity is concealed." He waves his fingers before his eyes and says, "Just blur out my face."

"But it's not the patient who's giving permission here," Taber says. "It's the next of kin, right?"

"We've talked to lawyers here and in New York," Barnes says, again placing his hand against his head. "It's been long established, in several legal cases over the last hundred years, that the right to privacy ends with death."

"I wasn't aware of that," Taber says. "But just because it's technically not illegal doesn't mean it's the right thing to do."

"We aren't required by law to obtain anyone's consent, especially if it's the kind of death that's already been covered by the news. We're doing it as a gesture of good will, so to speak."

"That's right," Michaelson says. "We have no legal obligation here."

Taber looks from Barnes to Michaelson, who stare back in quiet expectation, as if trying to guess the substance of his next argument.

"What about the families?" Taber says. "Will they be paid?"

"Two hundred dollars," Barnes says.

"It doesn't sound like much," Michaelson says, "but keep in mind that for documentaries and news reports, it's not customary for participants to be paid at all."

"It's a question of—how should I say it—*journalistic integrity*," Barnes says. "On the other hand, you can't expect them to do it for free."

Again Barnes raises his right hand to the back of his head. The gesture seems involuntary—perhaps some kind of tic.
Is he self-conscious about his baldness? Or about the mole on the back of his fleshy neck? His fingers caress his scalp, as if smoothing

the memory of hair. His massive torso rises and falls with each strained breath.

All at once Taber sees it: the uplifted hand has nothing to do with either his bald scalp or his mole. How did he not recognize it sooner? He wonders if Barnes feels tired, if he falls asleep at inopportune times. On autopsy, Barnes would probably have a dilated pulmonary artery.

Obesity makes hard work of breathing. A raised arm, by elevating his chest wall, lightens the burden on his diaphragm. Hypoventilation of obesity, also called Pickwickian syndrome: it was named for *The Pickwick Papers*. During his years in medical school, his wife Lizzie, an English major, enjoyed hearing about the occasional literary reference in medicine. She took particular delight in pointing out that it wasn't Pickwick but a minor character named Joe who was fat and oxygen-deprived.

III

HE SORTS THROUGH the week's mail, making a separate stack for the few items addressed to his dead wife. One of the envelopes he opens because of the hard edges inside, where a fake credit card is affixed to a letter bearing her name. He is inured to the refusal of banks and credit card companies to let death interfere with low interest solicitation.

His daughter's car appears in the window, and when she gets out he watches her tread through the ivy, stooping under the weight of her low-slung backpack. He goes to the door to let her in, but hesitates and listens to the scrape of her key in the lock. The thumbpiece twitches, the bolt clatters. They've had the same door her entire life, but whenever she comes home, she spends unnecessary seconds, even minutes, rediscovering the subtle method of lifting the handle while turning the key. He's given her different copies of the key, but always with the same result.

He imagines her outside on the doorstep, slouched shoulders and thick ankles. It bothers him that she can't seem to unlock the door. Does she have some kind of fine motor deficiency? He thinks of it as a matter of safety. What if she were being pursued by the pack of wild dogs that recently attacked a jogger down the street? Or the knife-wielding killer whose two victims Taber saw last month in the morgue?

Opening the door he says, "Knock and it shall be—"

"Whatever," she says and brushes past him and drops her stuffed backpack on the bottom stair. He notices small tears where the straps attach at the top of the backpack, but keeps from pointing out yet again that she doesn't need to carry so many books at the same time. The heavy backpack for some reason evokes feelings of tenderness and guilt.

"I think there's something wrong with the lock," he says. "We should look into getting it changed."

She stops at the hall table and shuffles through the mail, destroying his neat stacks. She doesn't seem to notice the junk mail addressed to her mother. He knows what she's looking for: a letter from Princeton, where she applied for early admission.

He follows her into the kitchen. She stoops in the light of the open refrigerator.

"I talked to Ken McGavin today," she says.

Taber is surprised by the surge of anger he experiences at the mention of the name. How ridiculous to harbor such feelings toward a teenager, someone else's child.

Her hand emerges from the refrigerator with a bag of miniature carrots.

"Did he come up with an excuse for not showing up?"

"He was actually really nice about it," she says, sticking a carrot into her mouth. "He was sick."

"How sick?"

"He was *incapacitated*," she says. From her solemn emphasis on this word, he assumes her to be under the mistaken impression that it somehow appeals to his medical sympathies.

"Did he go to the hospital?"

She shuts the refrigerator with more force than necessary, making the contents rattle.

With his last question he might have gone too far, but it seems she's too easily satisfied by the story. "Sick" could mean anything from a headache to mechanical ventilation. If he was too sick to pick up the phone, why didn't he just ask a family member to make the call? He's struck by her eagerness to believe something that doesn't make sense. She's too smart not to see the inconsistencies in Ken's story. She must have decided to ignore them, which means she's asking her father to ignore them as well.

Does she think she's in love? She's too young, she hardly even knows the guy. It's the kind of situation her mother would have known how to handle. The silence in the kitchen seems like an empty space her mother would have filled.

¶

Andrea sets the dripping bundle on the cutting board. She unfastens the clothes-pins and peels away the wet cloth. The brain belongs to Donald Anderson, the 32-year-old partly eaten by his pet dog. Preliminary lab tests indicate that he had HIV. On first exposure his brain had the consistency of egg yolk, but refrigeration and formaldehyde have restored to it a quality of life-like firmness— more like cool butter than living brain, but at least solid enough to cut with a knife.

Taber still doesn't know how Donald Anderson died. The body was discovered in a locked bathroom after neighbors complained of the smell. So horrified were police by the sight of the gore-plastered dog that they left it with the body in the bathroom and refused to go back until animal control had taken it away.

How long did the dog wait before starting to eat? Certainly longer than the beetles and maggots. It's not unusual for bodies to be consumed by house pets. Taber half remembers a morgue joke about an animal eating the hand that feeds it. In his experience, dogs tend to hold out longer than cats before eating their dead owners.

The death scene photographs, taken after the dog's removal, still hang on the bulletin board in the autopsy suite. Even if the dog hadn't chewed on Donald Anderson's face, the bloated discoloration would have made him totally unrecognizable. Large portions of his arms and legs had been eaten, including the bones of his hands and feet. There was no way to obtain fingerprints. The scene investigators confirmed his identity by matching the tattoos on his neck to the photograph on his driver's license.

Shriveled vessels lie in the grooves along the surface of his brain. Taber watches while Andrea cuts it in slices. Over the last few months she's become more facile with a knife. She uses a nine-inch, serrated blade of stainless steel and carbon. She pinches the hemispheres together with one hand and makes gentle sawing motions with the other. He admires the symmetry of the slices, the near uniform thickness.

The brain is riddled with tumors—glistening white and firm to the touch, the largest the size of a golf ball.

"What do you think?" he asks.

"Primary CNS lymphoma," she says. "Which happens to be my ex-husband's area of expertise."

She speaks as if the coincidence proved the diagnosis—and she's probably right—but they won't know for certain till samples have been fixed in paraffin, sliced thinner than paper, and stained with hemotoxylin, eosin, and silver.

"I didn't know you were married," he says.

"We separated last year, but only signed the papers a few days ago."

"I'm sorry to hear that."

"He seems to have fallen in love with somebody else."

He likes her use of *seems*, the amused resignation. He wants to tell her the guy was an idiot for choosing someone else, but he's reluctant to say anything she could take as flirtation.

"Sorry to bring it up," she says with a smile.

After the autopsy she stuffs her gown, gloves, and mask into the garbage bin. She has her hair pulled back, no make-up, and while she's attractive, her bloodshot eyes give an impression of stress and exhaustion.

Taber spends the next half-hour reviewing brain tumors online, specifically lymphoma in patients with HIV. He skims recent articles, some of which might have been co-authored by Andrea's ex-husband.

It's possible that Donald Anderson was a victim of some obscure poison or toxin not included on screening—that the brain tumors had nothing to do with his death—but Taber's instinct is to follow Occam's razor: the simplest solution is usually right. He'll offer a provisional report while he waits for the final lab results. His working hypothesis is that the brain tumors, most likely lymphoma, caused him to seize until he died.

Since there's no next-of-kin, Donald Anderson will be cremated at the expense of the state. Taber and Andrea have no obligation to be there, but he hates to think of an unattended funeral. He worries Andrea, as a fellow, might feel she has no choice, but she insists she was already planning to stay late.

It's the same priest they use for John and Jane Does: an old man willing to comply with state law by avoiding any mention of doctrine or deity. Taber and Andrea stand with the priest over a cardboard coffin. The smell persists, worse now, even though Donald Anderson's remains have spent a week in a freezer. Mixed with the putrefaction, Taber detects the formaldehyde from the brain. The priest rubs some kind of camphor ointment under his nose, which strikes Taber as a bit dramatic. He and Andrea listen to the secular bromides, then the three of them bow their heads for the inevitable moment of silence.

Afterward he sees white smoke over the roof and imagines particles of Donald Anderson drifting west over the Nashville skyline, and south over music row and even the apartment complex in Green Hills where neighbors remember him as quiet and polite, one of those weird guys who always kept to himself.

¶

Ken McGavin arrives on time, and with a bouquet of roses—presumably a dozen, but Taber doesn't stand there counting. He invites him in and the two of them face off in the living room, listening to the overhead sounds of Katie's preparation—clattering hangers, bursts of running water, and footfalls in between.

If nothing else, Ken seems to share Katie's taste in clothes: he wears black jeans and a black long-sleeved shirt. He has a splash of acne and a stud in his ear that at first glance Taber mistakes for an oily mole. Ken hunches forward in the cushioned chair. He pinches his knees together, perhaps to keep the bouquet from falling between his thighs. It rests in his lap, the buds pointing outward as if growing from his crotch. One of the petals drifts softly to the carpet. Taber wonders if he should take the flowers, maybe put them in water, but he has the sense that his daughter would enjoy receiving them directly from Ken. Besides, only Katie would know where to find a suitable container. He isn't sure they own an actual vase.

Taber points the remote control, but nothing happens, reminding him of the dying battery. Ken keeps his gaze fixed on the screen, as though by staring he might discover in it something more than his own reflection. Taber knows he should make conversation, but he's unsure of the etiquette, if such exists, for interrogating the suitor of one's daughter. He has no experience, this being the first time someone has come to the house to take her out.

What impression does he want to create in the mind of Ken McGavin? He wears a stern expression but can't imagine it having any impact. Intimidation doesn't come easily to him, if he's capable of it at all. Perhaps he should mention having her home on time. But what time would that be? He's never had any need to talk about a curfew.

"So Ken," he says, "what's your plan for tonight?"

"A movie?" he says. "Whatever Katie wants, I guess."

So he hasn't made any plan beyond the flowers. He grips the bouquet with both hands, like a baseball bat. Taber doesn't know what to make of the flowers. Do they represent some ironic throwback? A caricature of polite romance? Maybe it's simpler than that: maybe with the flowers he hopes to make amends for standing her up. Or maybe he's just trying to impress her old-fashioned father. Whatever the case, Taber is beginning to think the best way to discourage further cruelty is to treat him with kindness.

Ken is staring at the bookshelves.

"Most all the fiction and philosophy belonged to my wife," Taber says. "The medical texts and journals are mine."

"What kind of doctor are you?" Ken asks.

"I'm a pathologist."

"So you work in a laboratory?"

"Not exactly," he says. "I specialize in forensics, which means I spend most of my time doing autopsies."

"No way," he says with a flash of genuine interest, but then he looks away, and the acne speckling his cheeks momentarily blurs in a flush of red. Wrapping tissue crackles as he squeezes the bouquet in his lap.

"Have you ever heard of the body farm?" he asks.

"I did research there," says Taber. "We tried to date bodies based on the composition of insect populations."

"What kinds of insects do you find in bodies?"

"More than anyone knows," he says. "I was particularly interested in one called *Thanatophilus*, probably in part because of the name."

"What's that?"

"A type of beetle."

His lips turn in disgusted fascination.

"You might be interested in a new reality TV show called *American Autopsy*," Taber says.

"You're going to do autopsies on TV?"

"Not me," Taber says. "But some of the doctors I work with."

"That sounds like a really good show," he says.

A wire sprouting from his collar dangles an ear-piece. Taber wonders if the music apparatus is part of his daily attire, assuring a ready distraction in case of boredom. At least he isn't listening to music now, Taber thinks. But at the sound of Katie's footsteps on the stairs, the boy turns his head, and Taber sees the other bud lodged in his ear.

She wears all black—tights, skirt, sweater, and boots. The hem of her skirt is frayed, which worries Taber before he realizes it's intentional. Whether her clothes come from Goodwill or some expensive boutique, he has no idea, but he wonders if she has any sense of style whatsoever. Perhaps her teachers and classmates see her as a kind of charity case. Her outfits make him think of the chain-smoking inmates in the psychiatric hospital where he worked as a medical student.

Ken hands her the flowers. She sniffs them and says, "They're beautiful," and passes them to her father. Ken's hands have left the tissue crumpled and moist. Taber carries the flowers into the kitchen and sets them on the counter.

"So what movie are you going to see?" Taber asks.

Ken looks at Katie and shrugs. "What do you want to see?"

"I don't care," she says. She turns to her father and says, "We'll figure it out."

Taber watches them drop into either side of Ken's car, a Toyota Camry. Taber opens the door and jogs across the yard as Ken starts the engine.

"You know there's a recall on Toyotas," he says, "for faulty acceleration."

"Mine's too old," Ken says. "My dad looked into it."

Taber pats the roof of the car, as if to gauge some aspect of its design. All of a sudden the car lurches backward, nearly rolling over his foot. Ken slams on the brakes and pokes his head out the window and stares at him, as though anticipating some delayed manifestation of injury. Katie covers her face in a display of impatience and humiliation.

"Don't worry," Taber says. "I'm fine."

"I didn't realize how close you were," Ken says.

¶

The mechanical hum of the refrigerator seems to grow louder, as if to express his presentiment that Katie, at this very moment, is experiencing some form of humiliating cruelty. The dubious flowers still lie on the counter. Just waiting to die, he thinks.

He has no real concept of his daughter's social life, which till now seemed limited to the honor council and philosophy club. What do other 17-year-old girls do in their spare time? No doubt her lack of experience sets her apart from other girls her age. Has he gone too far in sheltering her, or has she simply inherited his tendency of social avoidance?

He's in no position to criticize, not when he puts so little effort into his own social life. He hasn't had a girlfriend in the four years since Lizzie died. An experiment in internet dating resulted in a few regrettable encounters, including a one-night stand with a nurse who in the morning confessed to having lied about her name and age on the website. Friends have expressed an interest in setting him up, but he's been reluctant to re-enter the fray in the year or so since his last blind date: a cousin of Michaelson's wife on the senatorial side.

He'd been impressed by her photograph, but the woman was even more beautiful in life. He'd numbed his anxiety beforehand with several mixed drinks, so it didn't take long for him to start slurring his speech. The low point came after dinner, when he returned from the bathroom only to have her point out the vomit on his sleeve.

He's rotating his third beer on the glass when he hears Katie's usual struggle with the front door. He lifts the beer and gulps the rest of it, nearly half the can.

The alarm gives a warning signal. In the hallway she punches the code into the console. The floor creaks as he steps up behind her. She turns with a start, and in her fleeting, unguarded expression he's reminded of her mother.

"How was it?" he says, uncertain if he wants to know the answer.

"Fine," she says, starting up the stairs. "I'm going to bed."

"What happened?" he asks. "You can tell me."

"All we did was a watch a movie—what else do you want to know?"

"Did you talk?"

"Of course," she says. "Do you think we spent three hours together without saying anything?"

He follows her upstairs, climbing at the same pace, as if drawn against his will by some invisible cord.

"Do you think you'll see him again?"

"We'll probably do something next week."

"Do something? Do what?"

Her eyes flicker with irritation as she withdraws into her bedroom.

"I just want to make sure you had fun," he says to the closed door.

Is it possible that Ken McGavin finds her physically attractive? Taber thinks of her face when she turned from the alarm panel, the startled expression that reminded him of Lizzie. Perhaps what

Ken McGavin sees is that hidden kernel of beauty. Or perhaps he's a rare, noble soul enamored by her intelligence and sense of humor. Other scenarios come to mind: he's a closet homosexual in need of a "girlfriend" to maintain a socially acceptable façade. He's a devoted Christian courting Katie not for himself but for Christ.

All at once he's wrenched by guilt: is it so hard to believe that someone would find his daughter attractive?

The facts of the case are simple enough: he stood her up but claimed he was sick. Since then they've gone to a movie, and supposedly there's another date in the works. Occam's razor points to the most straightforward solution—that he actually likes her.

IV

THAT SUNDAY MORNING TABER DISSECTS a homeless alcoholic found dead at the bus station downtown. With scissors he opens the stomach along its lesser curvature and finds the mucosal surface stained black and furrowed with swollen veins. It's clear the man died from gastric bleeding, the engorged veins a consequence of liver disease. He likely vomited the greater portion of his blood volume.

While Taber cuts the cirrhotic liver in slices, Chaquita peels the scalp from the skull, removing the face like a rubber mask. She cuts through the skull itself with an electric saw that fills the air with dry-smelling bone dust.

After clipping samples for microscopic analysis, he hefts the ravaged pieces of liver into a plastic bag Chaquita has placed between the cadaver's stiff legs. He takes one of the kidneys and weighs it on the scale. Then, pressing it against the cutting board, he saws through its long axis and opens it like a book.

Renalda, the scene investigator on call, comes in just as he places the brain on the cutting board. She holds up a sheaf of papers and announces that they have another autopsy. Taber is disappointed because he'd hoped to get home in time for a late lunch with Katie. He looks at the clock, and weighs the possibility of making the twenty-minute drive home before the next case, but it would be unfair to make Chaquita wait.

He goes rigid when he sees the name and age of the next cadaver written on the grease board: MCGAVIN, 17.

Taber sections the alcoholic's brain and arranges the paired slices flat on the cutting board. Then he lays down his knife and watches as Chaquita unzips a body bag and exposes Ken McGavin's pale face. He strolls to the counter, and clasping his gloved hands to his apron, reads Renalda's report. He died last night some time between one and two a.m. Emergency medical personnel found him bent around a tree more than twenty yards from his wrecked car.

He walks slowly around the table without touching him. An endotracheal tube juts from between the lips. On the chest he notices linear burns, the footprints of shock paddles. The only sign of trauma is an unnatural bend in the forearm, but he knows there are other fractures as well. The absence of proportionate bruising suggests he died not long after impact, if not immediately. So why was he intubated and shocked? Surely the paramedics knew he was already dead. Perhaps they saw it as an opportunity to practice their techniques. Taber has seen this before. Young paramedics need actual bodies to learn how to place chest tubes, endotracheal tubes, and central lines. On the other hand, if Ken McGavin's body were still warm, how could the paramedics have known with certainty that he was beyond resuscitation? Perhaps they realized the hopelessness of it in the ambulance on the way to the emergency room. Taber imagines the back of the ambulance, the persistent flat-line on the heart monitor. How long did they work before giving up and turning off the siren?

On Ken McGavin's right thigh is a tattoo: a cartoon character, the Road Runner, with spindly legs and feathers dragging streaks of color like contrails. He wonders what such an elaborate tattoo would cost. Did Ken's parents help him pay for it? He imagines a long argument, the parents enraged but eventually conceding: if it must be done, they insist on the highest standards of artistry and hygiene. And Ken, for his part, agrees to a location that would be covered by a bathing suit. Taber wonders if the Road Runner had some personal meaning to the boy, or if he just liked the way it looked on his thigh. But why a cartoon character? The attempt to imbue something inane with the weight of indelibility strikes Taber as uniquely adolescent.

He goes back to the alcoholic's brain. He scalpels tiny slivers into labeled plastic cassettes. Then he gathers into his hands the larger pieces of brain and drops them into the refuse bag. He removes his gloves and protective gear and washes his hands and then goes to the break room and pours a cup of coffee. The muted television, left on by Chaquita or maybe the janitorial staff, shows the preacher with the wrist tattoo. Is it a handcuff, as he previously assumed, or something else, a rosary perhaps?

He sips his coffee. He assumes Ken McGavin was under the influence of alcohol or drugs when he wrecked. He knows this will cause the family additional distress, but it might be the only thing to mitigate against suspicions of suicide. The weather was clear last night, the road conditions normal. He wishes he could remember the faces of Ken McGavin's parents. In his mind he apologizes to them. He is sorry for the enormous relief he feels that their son was alone when he died.

Ken's autopsy takes a little over an hour. He leaves blood smears on the greaseboard as he jots down the weight of each organ. He reminds Chaquita to be careful working in the chest near the sharp fragments of broken bone. She ladles almost three liters of blood from the chest cavity. She removes the heart along with the uppermost portion of the aorta. At the root of the aorta, where it attaches to the heart, he observes a small tear, less than a centimeter. It gives him quiet satisfaction to discover the precise mechanism of death. He carefully places the tip of his index finger through the tear and watches it emerge on the other side.

¶

He climbs the stairs and knocks on his daughter's bedroom door. At her desk she works on what looks to be her chemistry homework. She doesn't look up from her papers, even when he steps into the room and sits on her unmade bed.

The dried candle-wax on Katie's nightstand looks like a map of strange continents. The candle-wax has hardened at the base of a gold picture frame, fixing it in place. It's a photograph of her mother, taken perhaps twenty years ago.

"Ken McGavin died in a car accident," Taber says, keeping his voice low and even, drained of emotion.

She closes the textbook in her lap and turns and stares at him. He forces himself to hold her gaze. Tears form in her eyes and she looks away.

"Did you do an autopsy on him?" she asks.

"You know I can't say anything about that."

He goes to the bathroom and returns with a box of Kleenex. She takes one, wipes her eyes and cheeks, and then clenches it in her fist.

"Did he suffer?"

The usual question. Perhaps she heard it on television. He expects to receive the same inquiry from Ken McGavin's parents—or whoever else comes to identify the body.

"He died in an instant," he says.

But it seems to Taber that after bleeding out, Ken McGavin could have held on to some form of consciousness, at least for a brief time. Brain cells might survive without blood for two to three minutes, perhaps longer. At the moment of trauma, the surge of adrenalin and endorphins and the increased rate of neuronal firing might create a dilated experience of time. There's no way to know: it's impossible to subject this sort of question to the scientific method.

She's looking back at her book—not reading, just staring at the cover, absently thumbing a torn flap that hangs from the spine.

"You're going to be all right," he says.

She shrugs.

How much time had she spent with Ken McGavin, anyway?

A movie one night, perhaps lunch at school, and whatever minutes they might have found between classes. Surely not more than six hours in total. On the other hand, those six hours comprise the only romance she's ever experienced.

"There's something I need to know," he says. He wonders how best to ask the question, if he should ask it all.

"What?" she says. "What do you want to know?"

"Was Ken in your opinion a happy person?"

She stares at him and says, "He would never do that."

"I know," he says. "But he was alone when he died, so I have to ask."

What does he hope to gain, anyway? How could his daughter's opinion possibly affect his report? Even if she knew Ken well enough to assess his potential for suicide, she certainly wouldn't qualify as a reliable source.

Taber too has reason for bias. Did he not despise Ken McGavin for standing her up? Perhaps he despises him still. Would he favor suicide out of spite? Egregious misconduct, no doubt, but the mere possibility, however remote, is enough that he'd prefer to err on the side of calling it an accident. And he doubts anyone would fault him for doing so. He'd rather mistake a suicide for an accident than vice versa.

¶

The Center for Forensic Medicine occupies a new building in East Nashville, near the headquarters of the Tennessee Bureau of Investigation and the Department of Motor Vehicles. Visitors enter a large atrium with marble floors and generous skylights. There is an inscription in the marble over the doorway: *This is the place where death delights to succor life.*

Down the hall is a carpeted room with silk flowers, upholstered furniture, and serene paintings of landscapes. Here family members wait to identify their loved ones, whose faces appear on a television mounted on the wall.

Tina McGavin sits on the couch the Monday morning after her son's autopsy. Her eyes are bloodshot and swollen, but she smiles when Taber enters, tucks a Kleenex into her purse before shaking his hand. He recognizes her, presumably from church or some function at the University School.

Taber wears his white coat for occasions like this. He introduces himself, reminds her that his daughter was one of Ken's classmates.

"It's good to see you again," she says.

"I'm so sorry for your loss." He always uses the word so—perhaps meaningless, but somehow anchoring the rest of the sentence, preventing an easy slide into evasiveness or inadequacy. That she looks older than he remembers is due, he suspects, more to the toll of grief than the absence of make-up. She sits cross-legged, with her back straight and hands crossed at the wrists. Her purse gapes open on the small coffee table. Taber notices her wallet and keys, along with a canister of pepper-spray. Her gold bracelets clink as she tucks her hair behind her ears.

"I saw a guy down the hall with a video camera," she says.

"It's for a documentary TV show called *American Autopsy*."

"At the morgue?" she says. "Are you kidding me?"

"They weren't here when I examined Ken," he says.

"It sounds ridiculous," she says. "Who would want to watch a show about autopsies?"

"I can't imagine," he says. "I've been opposed to the idea from the very start."

"Nobody asked our permission to show Ken on TV," she says.

"And I can promise you he won't be."

He sits in the chair facing her. He rests his forearms on his thighs and waits for her to look at him, and when their eyes meet he says, "There was a tear at the base of his aorta—the largest artery in the body—just where it attaches to the heart."

"How did it tear?"

"Sudden deceleration," he says, "likely when his car made impact."

"Do you think he suffered?"

Not *Did he suffer?*, or *How long?*, but *Do you think he suffered?*

"I'm certain his death was instantaneous," Taber says.

She smirks and glances away. Does she perceive doubt in his voice? Perhaps she assumes he never equivocates over the question of suffering. Or like him, she's naturally suspicious when people tell her what she wants to hear.

"There are rare scenarios," he says, "where a victim of such an injury might remain conscious for a short time, if the bleeding from the aorta were contained somehow, perhaps by something called a pseudo-aneurysm, but I know for a fact that Ken died instantly."

He's speaking softly, almost whispering—the same voice he hears himself using sometimes in depositions, as if to keep the words themselves from obscuring the simple truth of what he's trying to say.

"There wasn't any superficial bruising," he says. "If he'd remained conscious, if blood had continued to circulate, even for mere seconds, contusions would have begun to form at the sites of injury."

A silence falls between them. He worries he might have given an impression of uncertainty, of a man desperate to convince himself of something he can't possibly know.

"Did Ken use drugs or alcohol?" he asks.

"No," she says. "He—"

She catches herself, looks away. He's seen this many times before

— the difficulty of avoiding the past tense.

"The wrestlers are obsessed with their diets," she says. "None of them drink or smoke or anything like that. Wrestling keeps those boys out of trouble."

Unless they're driving alone on a relatively straight road—completely sober as far as Taber can tell. But he won't know for certain until he receives the toxicology report.

"My husband's here with me," she says. "He's out in the car, he won't come inside."

"Would you like him to be here for the identification?"

She shakes her head and wipes the tears from her eyes and emits a brief snort, which Taber takes to be incompletely suppressed laughter.

After a pause, he says, "Are you ready, then?" She nods and takes a deep breath. He pulls the remote control from the pocket of his white coat and aims it at the television bolted to the wall.

The screen comes to life but shows only a bare, concrete floor.

He turns off the television and says, "Excuse me for just a moment."

Down the hall he finds Myra, one of the technicians, engrossed in the contents of some webpage of photographs and pastel wallpaper, but within seconds she closes the window.

Ken McGavin lies behind her, his face covered by a sheet.

Taber swallows and says, "Myra, please."

"That wasn't my login," she says. "I just turned on the computer and there it was."

"I don't care about the website," he says with a sigh. "I have the patient's mother in viewing."

Myra jumps to her feet, and Taber catches the back of her chair to keep it from knocking against the gurney. She rolls Ken's body under the camera. She bends down to make sure the front wheels of the gurney are parked at the markers, strips of duct tape on the floor. Taber pulls back the sheet and folds it neatly over Ken's chest. There's nothing he can do about the abrasions on Ken's cheeks and forehead, but he makes sure the scalp sutures are covered by hair.

He stops by Lakiesha's desk to retrieve the bulky, padded envelope that holds Ken's belongings. Through the window he notices a man in the parking lot, standing rigid, his hands in the pockets of his dark suit. He wears sunglasses and a red St. Louis Cardinals baseball cap.

Lakiesha shrugs and says, "He won't come in."

Tina McGavin hasn't moved from the couch. She doesn't look up when he enters. Her head is bowed, which makes him think she might be praying, so he stands in silence, holding the envelope at his side, until she looks up and meets his eyes.

"I'm sorry for the delay," he says.

He thumbs the power button on the remote control.

"Is this your son, Ken McGavin?"

She turns away from the screen, and with a nod mumbles, "It is, that's him, that's my son."

He switches off the monitor and offers her the envelope. "You'll find here some of Ken's belongings, the items he had with him last night when the ambulance arrived."

He has a mental image of the contents: wallet, belt, keys, pocket-change, iPod, and wrist-watch. Probably that earring he wore as well. He wonders if she'll go through the envelope or bury it in some drawer and leave it untouched for years, like a bedroom sealed and frozen in time.

She asks, "Did you happen to find our dog?"

"Dog?"

"Wilson, our golden retriever, was in the car with Ken." She peers into the envelope, as though searching there for some improbable sign of the missing animal.

"Are you sure?" he asks.

"When Wilson got agitated, Ken would take him for a drive."

"We didn't find him," Taber says. "I'm sorry."

She stands up. "I'm glad it was you," she says. "I thought I would have preferred it be a stranger, but I can tell that you cared about him. I know you treated him with—"

When it's clear she has no intention of finishing her statement, he says, "My daughter—and I'm sure everyone who had the privilege of knowing him—she's just devastated by this."

Taber escorts her into the foyer, and she leaves without saying anything more. Her husband takes off his hat as she approaches him on the concrete path. She laces her arm through his, but he seems reluctant to turn away from the building. He seems to be looking at something in particular, perhaps his own reflection, perhaps the outline of Taber's white coat hovering ghost-like behind it. They walk arm in arm across the parking lot. Just as they reach their Mercedes SUV, the husband turns again toward the morgue. He seems to weigh the possibility of going inside and seeing the body for himself. Ashamed, perhaps, that his wife had to do it alone. She clutches his forearm with one hand while caressing his back with the other. Taber sees her lips moving. He thinks she might be saying, "I know, I know."

¶

Katie lies on the couch with Augustine's *CONFESSIONS*, which she's reading for her World Religions class.

"It might be time to go back to school tomorrow," he says. "You've stayed home two days now."

"I don't know," she says without taking her eyes from the page.

"I'm surprised how hard you're taking it," he says.

She sets down the book. "Do you honestly think I'm using this as an excuse to cut school?"

"Absolutely not," he says. "That's not what I'm saying. I just think you might benefit from talking about it with your friends and teachers, and the counselors at school. Everyone in your class is dealing with this."

"They didn't know anything about him," she says.

The last thing he wants is to belittle her grief. He recently heard a scientist on NPR ascribe the emotional instability of teenagers to incomplete myelination of the frontal lobes. Perhaps her disproportionate reaction to Ken McGavin's death is an effect of frontal lobe immaturity: electrical impulses traveling in faulty loops instead of being transmitted to the appropriate processing points. Perhaps it's the very confusion of such impulses that forces the brain, eventually, into a higher level of organization.

"Did you check the mail today?" he asks.

"No," she says, surprising him, because any day now she could hear from Princeton.

He goes outside, and as he walks back from the mailbox, he shuffles through the stack.

"Nothing," he says.

"Listen to this," she says, with her book opened to an underlined passage. "'If an infant does no harm, it is not for lack of will, but for lack of strength.'"

"A little harsh," he says.

"How many direct ancestors does one person have?" she asks. "If I go back x generations, each generation being thirty years, that's two to the power of x people in that generation alone. Going back to the beginning of time—it would be a number beyond calculation. What is the probability of at least one of those people being a murderer or rapist?"

"There's no way to know."

"One hundred percent," she says, tapping her fist against her thigh. "It's a statistical certainty that every man and woman on earth is a descendant of rapists and murderers."

He approves of her mathematical approach to original sin, but hates to hear her using such bleak terms.

"If what you're saying is true," he says, "then maybe the good in the world is proof for the existence of God."

The good in the world? How empty he sounds when he tries to channel Lizzie's optimism. This idea of ancestral rape and murder wouldn't have even crossed her mind if her mother were alive. He suspects she was thinking like this even before Ken's death. Perhaps he shouldn't be so surprised by her cheerless view, since every day he brings home thoughts of violence and cruelty. Is it possible that such notions, never verbalized, still pass to his daughter like some kind of infection?

V

AS HE WALKS UP the steep driveway, laughter emanates from the lighted windows of Michaelson's large Tudor house. A pair of valet parking attendants wait outside the four-car garage. Perhaps they're offended at the sight of Taber coming up the hill on foot, but he restrains an impulse to apologize. It seems ridiculous to offer valet parking at a house party, even if your guests include the makers of a reality TV show.

Anna Michaelson greets him in the foyer. "It's so good of you to come," she says, hardly turning from a woman he doesn't recognize. "You can leave your coat in the guestroom."

He makes his way down the hall and adds his coat to the pile on the bed. He can't recall when he last visited the Michaelsons—maybe the previous year's holiday party. Lizzie died before they moved into this house, but she would have been amused by the extravagance. She'd have pointed out the antique bedframe and dresser, the plantation shutters, and the granite counter and polished fixtures in the bathroom. He can almost hear her whispering, *"How much did that cost?"*

He follows the sound of voices to the living room, where Tamagi and Landman pluck hors d'œuvres from a tray on the mantel. The man across from them wears a monogrammed shirt and pleated pants. His thin tie is speckled with tiny, brown-skinned figures playing saxophones. He stands in the path to the bar, leaving Taber no choice but to make conversation.

"Just in town from New York," the man says. "I manage the financial side of things at 8th Window Productions."

Landman curls her lips into a rare smile. "We were just talking about some of the cases that might have made AMERICAN AUTOPSY if they'd started filming just a few weeks earlier."

"Where was I?" Tamagi asks, clearly annoyed to have been interrupted by Taber.

"The body had been scrubbed clean by the murderer," says the man with the tie.

"Right," says Tamagi. "The key was the raw oysters in the stomach. Nobody knew who she'd been with that night, but not many places in Nashville serve raw oysters. The cops went to every restaurant on that list with pictures of the victim."

Landman looks at Taber. "You remember that case?"

"Sorry," he says, though he remembers it well. His reticence probably comes across as self-righteous, but he isn't sure the rules of confidentiality should be discarded for anyone remotely affiliated with *AMERICAN AUTOPSY*.

As he nears the bar, he overhears Landman behind him: "We aren't talking specifics here, just the general themes of the case."

The irritation in her voice makes him wonder if he went too far. He didn't intend any kind of overt reprimand—all he said was sorry—but she probably took it that way, and the presence of the TV executive likely made it worse.

He orders a gin and tonic. Michaelson's in-house bar consists of a small vestibule off the kitchen, with a window facing the living room. The bartender looks like he might be in college, perhaps one of the Vanderbilt tennis players Michaelson supports with scholarship donations and summer internships. Himself a former player, he follows their matches with a devotion that borders on fanatical. His charity occasionally takes the form of hiring the team members for easy housework at exorbitant hourly rates.

The kid at the bar is picking up bottles and reading labels, which confirms his amateur status in the field of bartending. Taber helps by pointing out the gin. A few banknotes sagging from a pint glass invite tips, but all he has in his wallet is a twenty-dollar bill.

Michaelson leans against the back of the couch, his arms crossed, nodding at whatever Barnes is saying. Taber starts in their direction but his drink, filled to the brim, spills at the slightest motion. Michaelson and Barnes watch as he sips it down to a safe level. He winces at the taste, almost pure gin, and wonders if the kid added any tonic at all. He goes back and leaves the twenty-dollar bill on the bar.

"We were just discussing your protégée," Michaelson says.

"Whether or not she's competent to make her own decisions," Barnes adds.

Last week Andrea admitted that Billy, the cameraman, had been so brazen as to film her outside of work, even while she swam laps at the Y. Taber protested in an email to Barnes and Michaelson, proposing limitations to Andrea's involvement, but neither bothered to reply.

"Who wouldn't want to be on a great TV show?" Michaelson asks.

"I don't know what she wants," Taber says. He can't implicate Andrea as the source of complaint—not while she's still in training and hoping for a job offer.

"No one's forcing her to participate," Michaelson says, stabbing the ice in his glass with a stirrer.

"Then stop filming her," Taber says.

Barnes takes a step back and holds up his hands in mock surrender. Taber finds it irritating, this strategy of engendering conflict by pretending to be threatened.

"Let's everyone just calm down," Michaelson says, with a conciliatory laugh that seems to further the idea of Taber's volatility.

"My point is," Taber says, "she might not feel like she has a choice. It's the same reason residents and fellows aren't allowed to be subjects in research protocols. Clearly this is a far cry from a drug trial, but because it's a project involving her superiors, she's not in a position to refuse."

"The show could be a great opportunity for Andrea," Michaelson says.

"It would be a shame not to make the most of that thirty-something sex appeal," Barnes says, "but at least we got her in a swimsuit. The money shot, if you will."

Taber feels a tightening behind his eyes. His hand shakes as he raises his glass to his mouth. Michaelson tries to relieve the silence with a courteous chuckle.

"You'll have to get Andrea's permission to use whatever footage you have," Taber says, making little effort to keep the anger out of his voice.

"Already done," Barnes says. "She signed every form we put in front of her."

He excuses himself and squeezes his massive bulk between an armchair and houseplant. He pushes aside the thin branches, causing leaves to fall to the floor.

Michaelson takes a step closer to Taber—as if to set the tone for greater honesty now that Barnes is gone—and says, "You feel strongly about this whole business with Andrea."

"As the de facto program director," Taber says, "I don't think our fellow should have the responsibility of bringing *sex appeal* to the morgue."

"You wouldn't deprive her the opportunity to be part of the show just because she's beautiful."

"Why not just wait till she's a partner?" he asks. His eyes drift over a family of Herend rabbits gathered at the base of a candlestick. "And in July, when she's signed a contract, ask her what kind of role she wants in *AMERICAN AUTOPSY*.

"You talk as if the job offer were a foregone conclusion," Michaelson says. "But frankly I'm not convinced she's a team player."

"Because she doesn't like prancing around in a bathing suit for a TV show?" Taber realizes he's whispering. He clears his throat and in a voice only slightly louder says, "She's the most qualified applicant we've ever had. Did you see her score on the in-service?"

"Look," he says, "we've been friends a long time, and I don't want to play games here. I like Andrea as much as anyone, but when it comes down to it, education isn't the primary purpose of the Forensic Group. Our involvement in this show, regardless of how you feel about it, could yield large profits for us, as a group, and if Andrea's going to stay around, I need to know that she supports what we're doing."

Taber turns away without responding.

"Everything's going to be fine," Michaelson says, but Taber, refusing even to look at him, retreats toward the nearest door.

He grips his car keys in his pocket, the metal digging into his palm. His hand unclenches only after the door closes between him and Michaelson.

A woman in an apron and chef's hat sprinkles coriander on a tray of deviled eggs. She looks at Taber with polite curiosity. He has the sense of having stumbled backstage during a play.

On the opposite side of the kitchen, a swinging door gives way to a dim passage with a staircase ahead and bedrooms on either side. The bedrooms belong to Michaelson's kids—in just a glance he can tell—but the usual teenage clutter, along with the teenagers themselves, seems to have been gathered up and hidden from sight.

His eyes are drawn to a framed photograph in one of the bedrooms. From a crowd of trophies, gold figurines seem to watch as he pads across the freshly vacuumed carpet. The state champion wrestler is in Katie's class, but as far as Taber knows, the two of them hardly interact.

He starts at the sight of a cat reclining on the taut bedcovers. Perfectly still, its haughty, accusatory gaze evokes a sudden awareness of impropriety. He has no business in the boy's room—the door wasn't left open as an invitation for guests to peruse.

The picture shows the Michaelson family, all five of them, on some treeless mountain, a panorama of craggy peaks in the background. The skinny twin daughters pose in an attitude of celebration. Michaelson stands with an arm draped over the broad shoulders of his son. The family looks beautiful, delighted by their athletic prowess in climbing the mountain. The photograph seems to equate family affection with grueling conquest. Taber examines the daughters' faces, but can't tell if the photograph was taken before or after the nose jobs they supposedly received for their eighteenth birthday.

Also hanging on the wall is a photograph of the University School wrestling team—three rows of boys in matching sweat suits. Some have wrestling headgear dangling at their thighs. All but one of the tiny faces express scowls. Why does this one boy, out of all of them, choose to smile? Does he hope to stand out among his teammates—perhaps to demonstrate a contrarian lack of seriousness? Or is it merely the boy's habit, quaint and possibly naïve, to smile for every photograph? All at once Taber realizes he knows him: the smiling boy is Ken McGavin.

Down the hall, in the dining room, he finds Andrea spooning liquid cheese onto a plate of tortilla chips. She looks at him and smiles. Taber takes one of the plates and circles the smorgasbord laid out on the dining room table.

"I'm surprised no one's filming you while you eat," he says.

"You never know." She reverts here head as if checking for a camera.

They can see through the doorway into the living room, where most of the guests are gathered. Taber notices a black woman in her forties, sipping a glass of wine near the fireplace. There is a slight bulge to one of her eyes—most obvious when she looks down at her glass, when the exposed white gleams above the iris.

"That woman has proptosis," he says as he bites into a stuffed mushroom.

"Thyroid disease?" Andrea suggests, but finding the woman in question, says, "That would be unusual in a single eye. The demographics might point to sarcoid."

Taber makes eye contact with the woman and looks away. Does she know they're talking about her?

"What else?" he asks.

"Lymphoma," she says. "I'd also think about mets—and maybe orbital pseudotumor or Wegener's, though there's no evidence of preseptal inflammation."

She holds the plate under her chin as she bites into the first of her chips. She only notices the dollop of cheese on her dress when Taber offers his napkin. By wiping it, she smears the cheese over a larger area.

He follows her into the kitchen and she opens the freezer and takes a piece of ice and presses it against the stain. Taber glances at the caterer, who looks on with skeptical amusement, as if doubting the very idea of using ice on a cheese stain.

He can tell Andrea is still thinking about the differential diagnosis for proptosis.

"Any other ideas?" he asks.

"Glioma, meningioma, hemangioma, hemangiopericytoma, and fibrous histiocytoma."

When Andrea began her fellowship, Taber was reluctant to test her knowledge like this. In medical school, he had several attendings who seemed to delight in riddling him with questions he had no hope of answering. Medical students and residents referred to this sort of Socratic interrogation as "pimping." The purpose of pimping, it seemed, was to squelch unfounded pride. Taber had resolved to treat Andrea as a colleague rather than an underling, which meant she'd be spared the casual humiliation of being pimped. But early on, in one of the weekly meetings Taber scheduled to discuss her progress, she surprised him by actually complaining about the lack of pimping. He's come to realize that she genuinely enjoys being quizzed, no doubt because she knows every answer. Taber now finds himself researching topics for the sole purpose of pimping Andrea, and still he has trouble reaching the boundaries of what she knows.

Like him, she failed to take advantage of the free valet parking. So they walk together down the hill, leaning back to compensate for the incline. She grips Taber's arm for balance. She takes small steps on her elevated heels, and her grip tightens on the steeper parts of the hill.

The unusually strong gin and tonic has left a vague numbness in the skin of his face. Touching his own cheek, he has the impression of an intervening membrane, the thinnest of masks.

¶

The staff gathers in the conference room to watch the first episode of *AMERICAN AUTOPSY*. Michaelson passes out green baseball caps with the Science Channel's logo. Taber adjusts his to the largest size, but when it still doesn't fit, he folds it over and stuffs it in his back pocket.

Aaron Barnes stands and waits for the room to go silent. "I want to welcome you all on behalf of 8th Window Productions—and to tell you how excited we are about *AMERICAN AUTOPSY*.

He glances around the room, briefly making eye contact with Taber. Then he shrugs and says, "So without further ado."

Taber smiles at the applause that follows. Chaquita pokes her fingers in her mouth and whistles. Myra pumps her fists. For all his deliberation, he hasn't until this moment considered the show's impact on his staff. Under normal circumstances, Chaquita calls in sick at least once every couple of weeks, but she hasn't taken a single day off since filming began.

The opening credits flash over a montage of urban nightscapes—rushing highways, dilapidated buildings, a littered alleyway sealed off by yellow tape. Police lights paint a body bag as it's loaded into the back of an ambulance.

The credits, in old-fashioned Courier, have an animated quality, such that the names appear to shake like muscles held in tension. The intended effect is presumably one of suspense—the text literally shaking with fear—but Taber has an impression of strain and instability.

In raspy voice-over, a narrator describes the basic facts of the case: "When the decomposed body of a 23-year-old woman surfaces in scenic Radnor Lake, police look to Dr. Brandt Michaelson to ascertain the cause of death."

The pale corpse lies bloated in an autopsy basin, the breasts and genitalia blurred. Taber shakes his head, amused by the show's decision to depict stab wounds but censor nudity.

The scene cuts between the autopsy suite and an interview with Michaelson, no single shot lasting more than a few seconds. The victim's back-story is suggested by bucolic shots of trees and grass. In a blurred re-enactment, she and her boyfriend hold hands on a wooded path. Apparently, he stabbed her in a jealous rage and then filled her clothes with stones and sank her body in the lake. Foreboding music accompanies shots of lake water rippling in moonlight.

Michaelson sits with a panel of microscopes in the background, speaking about the difficulty of estimating the time of death. He describes how in this case the lake water slowed the process of decomposition.

Now he's back in the autopsy suite, gesturing with his scalpel.

"The unusual whiteness of the body is caused by what we call adipocere," he says. "This is what happens to fat in cold water."

The camera makes him look like an inaccurate replica of himself. It's partly an effect of his make-up, likely the same mask he's worn for his various appearances on the local news, but there's also something about the lighting, or perhaps the pixilation of digital photography, that gives a strange impression of counterfeit flesh, like an android in a science fiction movie.

Chaquita moves in the background with her usual efficiency. The camera catches her rolling her eyes—at least that's how it looks to Taber—when Michaelson says, "I sometimes think of myself as a customs officer on the River Styx." Taber glances around at the still figures in the dark room and finds Chaquita sitting against the wall, staring at the screen with a blank expression.

Cut from the autopsy suite to Andrea discussing the importance of a "well-rounded lifestyle." In voice-over she says, "Exercise reminds us that we're alive." There are shots of Michaelson on his mountain bike, Landman playing tennis, and Tamagi in some yoga position. The exercise montage culminates with the so-called money shot—Andrea climbing out of a pool. Taber glances over just as she buries her face in her hands.

The show tries to create an element of human interest by portraying the marriage of two forensic pathologists. When an interviewer asks Giles Tamagi which of them is the better pathologist, he says, "I am, of course." There are chuckles around the room, though it's clear he isn't making a joke. In a separate interview, his wife, Karen Landman says, "It's interesting how his over-confidence occasionally makes up for his intellectual shortcomings."

Tamagi has a trauma victim with extensive chemical burns on the face and arms. The 22-year-old male was driving on the highway with supplies for his meth lab. In the passenger seat, his inebriated girlfriend held in her lap a bucket of a volatile chemical, anhydrous ammonium. When she spilled the bucket, the car instantly filled with noxious fumes, scorching their skin and eyes. The driver opened his door and tumbled from the vehicle at eighty miles per hour.

Taber remembers the case. The girlfriend died as well, but her family must not have signed the permission forms.

Tamagi stands over the body and with a ballpoint pen indicates the burns on the face, neck, and forearms. It reminds Taber of a magician waving his wand over a person about to be sawed in half.

The victim's mother identifies the body. She has bloodshot eyes and ragged clothes, and when she opens her mouth and wails, "That's my baby," Taber can see the brown stubs of teeth behind her wrinkled lips. Taber has heard about meth addicts pawning everything they own to satisfy the craving. How easy it must have been to convince this woman to sign the forms—two hundred dollars for the spectacle of her tragedy.

VI

KEN MCGAVIN'S TOXICOLOGY screen comes back negative, which authenticates his reputation for clean living but in no way resolves the lingering question as to the manner of death.

Taber drives to the site of the wreck—a segment of Chickering Road lined on one side by mansions and on the other by the dense foliage of Percy-Warner Park.

He pulls onto the curb and switches on his hazards. He's struck by the house across the street: a kind of modernist sculpture, an architectural experiment dominated by a massive upside-down cone.

An argument dies the moment it forms, that Ken might have been distracted by the house. But of course he wouldn't have been able to see it, not at night. It occurs to Taber that he's grasping for a reason to write off this death as an accident.

He unfolds a printed sheet with several photographs: the crumpled hood, the hole in the windshield.

Ken was driving north, toward Belle Meade at eighty to ninety miles an hour. The weather was clear. There is in fact a gentle curve in the road, but not enough to explain the loss of control, even at those speeds. There are no skid marks, which means he didn't slam on the brakes before impact.

Did he spill a drink in his lap, or reach to the floor for his dropped phone? Did he have a seizure?

Perhaps he was distracted by the dog, the golden retriever his mother mentioned. But where is the dog now? Taber can't imagine it surviving the crash and climbing out of the vehicle through the hole in the windshield.

The question draws him back to Occam's razor. The truth lies in the simplest explanation, which is Ken must have let out the dog. He must have intended to crash.

A patch of bare earth stands out against the surrounding mat of leaves. He spots bits of glass in the dirt, and on the nearby pavement as well. The tree-trunk bears gashes from the impact. Embedded in the wood is a shard of translucent plastic, a piece of a headlight.

That night he's on his third beer when he logs on to the Forensic Group's network and pulls up his draft of Ken McGavin's autopsy report. All that remains is the manner of death, accident or suicide. But he's unlikely to find definitive proof of suicide. The real choice comes down to accident or undetermined.

The University School directory sits on his desk. He could phone the McGavins for more detail on the dog. Maybe Brian, the father, remembers a different sequence of events. Did they actually see the dog in the car? Maybe it merely ran away and Ken left in the car to search for it. Of course if they altered their story at this point Taber would have to assume they'd realized the implications and decided to lie.

Perhaps another car was involved—perhaps he swerved to avoid a head-on collision with a drunk driver. Or it might have been a seizure, presumably his first: there's no mention of epilepsy in the medical record. His brain was normal on autopsy, but those of epileptics usually are.

He finishes his beer and lays his head against the desk. He considers the parents, how it would pain them if he left open the possibility of suicide.

Could Ken have suffered major depression without his parents' knowing? Surely there were signs, signs they of all people would have noticed. And if they'd had the slightest suspicion he might have been depressed, would his mother have been so foolish as to mention that dog? Grief can no doubt make people irrational, but at the time of the identification, she'd known of his death for almost twenty-four hours, more than enough time to consider the possibility that he'd stopped to let out the dog. That she mentioned it at all might support the opposite conclusion: that he wasn't depressed and therefore couldn't have killed himself. There are gaps in this line of reasoning—he sees them even now, tired as he is and maybe a little drunk—but the gaps seem trivial next to the strange pleasure he takes in deriving opposite conclusions from the same piece of evidence.

Nothing worse than losing a child, but why should the parents' grief factor into his decision? Or his own need to make amends for hating the boy? How is it that he so easily accepts this bias? The parents he knew, the victim a kid he despised. He would have recused himself from the case had it not been a Sunday.

He writes ACCIDENT and signs the report. He can't prove it, but there was no life insurance, so it's unlikely he'll ever have to.

¶

The next day he finds Katie watching *AMERICAN AUTOPSY*, recorded on DVR while she was at school. When she was little she wanted to visit the morgue, but Taber never allowed it. It's been a long time since she showed any interest in seeing his work.

On TV Tamagi points out the abrasions and chemical burns on his patient's skin. It's vaguely disorienting for Taber to see a cadaver in his living room. Cold water trickles against stainless steel between the dead man's feet—so familiar, yet he never imagined these things invading his very home.

He glances at Katie and imagines the cadaver projected on her retinas and fragmented into hundreds of billions of electrical impulses traveling through her brain and altering membrane receptor configurations, not just in the visual cortex but in the parietal and temporal lobes and limbic system as well—the deep, unconscious parts of her brain that spawn dreams and associations.

"I kind of feel sorry for Dr. Tamagi," she says. "Even though he's a total freak. His wife said on TV that he looks like a court jester in his yoga gear."

"I'm sure she means well," says Taber.

"What's funny is that it's an accurate description."

"You don't have to watch this," he says. "In fact, I'd rather you didn't."

She turns on the couch and looks at him. "Are you offended?"

"No," he says, smiling. "But the sooner it goes off the air, the better."

"You're not even on it," she says. "I mean, anybody in their right mind would rather watch you than Dr. Tamagi."

"Let's just say the director and I have creative differences."

The victim's mother is talking about highway safety when Taber notices the envelope on the coffee table with the familiar black and orange emblem from Princeton. When he reaches for it Katie complains that he's blocking her view, but he can tell she's holding back a smile. By the time he finishes reading her acceptance letter, she's paused the TV show, fixing an image of Tamagi's face in an attitude of haughty perplexity. Taber notices a pair of blurred figures in the background—himself and Andrea hunched over some specimen.

"Dad," she says, "I won't qualify for financial aid."

"That doesn't make any difference," he says. "It's not something you should even think about."

The money from Lizzie's insurance policy collects minimal interest in a savings account. Taber looks forward to being rid of it. He remembers when the insurance representative came to the house to deliver the check, the same man who had sold them the policy ten years earlier. Three hundred thousand dollars—Taber had never seen a check for so much money.

He hasn't spent any of it, but there is security in knowing it's there. It bothers him to have profited from the death of his wife, and the monthly statements still evoke feelings of guilt. He once considered giving it all to St. Bernard's, the Episcopal church where he claims membership. No question it's what Lizzie would have wanted. But instead he gave the church the standard ten percent, above and beyond the ten percent from his monthly paycheck.

Sometimes it seems like his religious life has become a matter of accounting. He has no natural faith, no conviction. After years of low intensity churchgoing, why hasn't he, like Lizzie, been overcome by an upwelling passion? The most convincing argument he's ever heard for belief is Pascal's wager. However implausible heaven and hell, the stakes are too high to risk, so one might as well believe. Perhaps simplistic, but given the number of children who die every day, it seems perfectly reasonable that God would recommend Himself in terms even a child could understand. And yet, Taber can't recall Pascal's wager ever bringing him the slightest inspiration or comfort.

A memory takes hold: a note his wife jotted in a book.

Katie resumes *AMERICAN AUTOPSY* while he browses the book-lined shelves. His eye goes to a gap in one of the rows, a dark space between two hardbacks. A gap just wide enough for his index finger. He pulls out the small, tattered paperback copy of *THE SICKNESS UNTO DEATH*. Her favorite book in college, she read it so many times that vertical creases in the spine have almost completely effaced the print.

Only after she died did he take the time to read it. He found himself, not surprisingly, more interested in her marginal notes than in the text itself.

He's annoyed to hear himself on television saying, "We take what we do very seriously."

"Look at you," Katie says, but he doesn't bother looking.

He flips through the yellowing pages—careful not to cause further tears—till he finds the bit of marginalia that struck him four years ago.

In the blank space at the end of a chapter Lizzie wrote: "Each person must face the unknown something that her anxiety points her to, and thus answer the highest demand that can be made of her: to complete the self by succumbing to the hand of God, or to negate the self perpetually and unsuccessfully."

VII

A MAN STRIDES UNINVITED into Taber's office and hands him a manila envelope and says, "You've been served." The envelope is blank except for his name typed in the center. The man too is a kind of blank—gone too quickly to leave an impression beyond that passive-aggressive cliché of the court, aggression in the passive voice. He cringes at the distorted notion of *service*. Despite countless depositions and appearances in court, Taber has only heard those three words spoken on television.

With shaking hands he unfastens the clasp and draws out the sheaf of papers. He scans over the state seal, the words "Superior Court of Davidson County".

He thinks: *I'm being sued.*

His mind races through recent cases—questionable calls he made, the few times family members have requested that his autopsy findings be reviewed by another pathologist.

The plaintiffs, named on the right side of the top page, are Tina and Brian McGavin. It takes him a moment to place the names. Why would they sue? He would understand if he'd recommended suicide, but he called their son's death an accident.

The list of defendants runs over to the second page. It includes all of the pathologists in the group, even Andrea Gill. Also listed is Aaron Barnes, along with several names he doesn't recognize. The McGavins are suing the Forensic Group as well as 8th Window Productions and the Science Channel.

Did Ken McGavin's body appear on *AMERICAN AUTOPSY*?

A message flashes on his computer screen: Michaelson wants to see him immediately.

Taber steps into the hallway, reading as he walks. He's only vaguely aware that he's heading toward the bathroom, not even sure why he's going there. He stares at the block paragraphs of legalese.

As far as he can tell, there are four accusations, each presented in bold font, and followed by several explanatory paragraphs.

1. Interference with or mishandling of human remains.
2. Invasion of privacy based on intrusion upon seclusion.
3. Invasion of privacy for publicizing private facts.
4. Infliction of emotional distress.

The first of the charges disturbs him most. His eyes linger on one particular phrase: *abuse of a corpse*. He's heard of the statute on mishandling human remains. He always thought it applied only to depraved crimes like grave robbery and necrophilia.

Do these lawyers really believe he or his partners would exploit a teenager's body for what the document refers to as "ghoulish entertainment?" And while perhaps reprehensible, would any reasonable judge or jury consider it abuse? Abuse of a corpse?

He knows Tina McGavin. Their children were friends. More than friends. It's shocking that she would think him capable of such an atrocity.

He remembers the day she identified the body of her son—the awkwardness of the TV monitor. At the time, he thought of it as a glitch, a misstep in a delicate performance. How much simpler things were when he and Michaelson worked at Metro General, where the dead were identified through a plate-glass window.

What did she see, anyway? Ken couldn't have been shown on television. Even if Taber had agreed for once to admit the cameras—even if the McGavins had given permission—the crew was nowhere to be found on the Sunday morning of Ken's autopsy.

On the off chance that his body was filmed the following day, before he was taken to the funeral home, the footage should have been either destroyed or stored in a confidential file like any photograph from an autopsy or death scene.

He wonders if she could have mistaken another body for that of her son. She saw the camera that day. Death gradually erodes all distinguishing features, and in the earliest stages, even before the onset of decomposition, there is a blurring of individuality. Two faces, dissimilar in life, might look strangely alike in the death.

He locks the bathroom door and turns on the faucet and washes his face. It doesn't bother him that water splashes onto the documents he's placed on the counter. When he's composed himself, he goes back out into the hallway, and peers into the autopsy suite, empty but for a single cadaver awaiting transport to some funeral home or cemetery.

A heavy silence, though no quieter than usual—he's just more aware of it.

Andrea is sitting in near darkness, reading the court summons by the glow of her computer screen. Thin bars of light stretch over the empty cubicles closest to the louvered windows. She turns away when Taber enters. When she looks at him he can tell she's been crying.

"Do you remember seeing Ken McGavin on the show?" he asks.

She shakes her head and blows her nose into a scrap of tissue. He takes a box of Kleenex from one of the empty cubicles and sets it on her desk.

"Should I call a lawyer?" she says. "I can't afford a lawyer."

"These accusations," he says, waving the papers. "I'd be willing to swear there was no sign of Ken McGavin on that show."

She takes the summons into her lap and holds it with a kind of strange tenderness, rubbing the edges with her thumbs.

"Abuse of a corpse," she says. "It's such an awful phrase."

"There's certainly no reason you should be included here."

"I'm as much a part of that show as anyone else."

"You're in training," he says. "Everything you do here is our—my responsibility. I'm going to do everything in my power to get your name removed from this."

"This is something I'll have to explain every time I apply for a state license or hospital credentials."

"I don't think so," he says. "I'm not sure it's even a valid case."

"There you are," Michaelson says from the doorway. He cinches his tie against his throat, as if preparing for an audience.

"Let's see what this is all about," he says, removing a DVD from its box.

They watch the show on the computer in Andrea's small cubicle. She has to back her chair against the partition when Michaelson, seemingly oblivious to how much space he occupies, sits on her desk.

Taber studies the cadavers in the background. None of the bodies bear any resemblance to Ken. He assumes the McGavins have made a mistake. Perhaps they glimpsed some anonymous body part, a hand or foot attached to their son by nothing more than their desire to see him.

Several times Taber focuses on a possible candidate, only to find some obvious discrepancy, like grey hair or breasts. It's toward the end of the episode that he finally sees it. He's certain of it even before they rewind. During a brief interview with Andrea, a corpse lies on a gurney parked behind her. The face and genitals are blurred, but not the cartoon on Ken McGavin's thigh. The Road Runner seems to be charging upward, on a collision course with Andrea's elbow. There's no mistaking it for a bruise or birthmark.

The money shot, Taber thinks. How did no one notice it that day in the conference room, or later when the show aired on television? His impulse is to blame the editor, who perhaps after staring so long at cadavers and middle-aged pathologists found himself mesmerized by Andrea, her telegenic appeal at that moment too strong even for his professional duty to scrutinize the background for narrative inconsistencies or potential sources of litigation.

¶

A headline on the front page of *The Tennessean* reads LAWSUIT COULD KILL MORGUE SHOW.

The article gives the impression that Michaelson courted the production company with promises of horrific death. Early in 2009, he sent the producers several emails describing at least two cases—a teenager beaten to death with a baseball bat and a sky-diver whose parachute failed to open.

Taber cringes to read it. No doubt the reporter has seen the actual email messages. That Michaelson would use someone's death as a kind of sales pitch—it seems to Taber a gross violation of ethics, though perhaps no worse than the show itself.

The article claims it was important to Michaelson that the show feature his family at their Belle Meade home. The reporter describes it as a "mansion," which seems to Taber somewhat misleading, though in keeping with the depiction of Michaelson as a heartless profiteer.

Did Michaelson have a film-crew at his house? Taber wouldn't be surprised. After all, there was a camera on Andrea even while she swam laps at the Y.

Apparently he wanted the show to launch acting careers for his 19-year-old twin daughters. Taber is amazed that Michaelson would admit such an outrageous motive. Or did the reporter obtain this information from another source? Michaelson's wife perhaps, or someone at the production company.

Taber receives messages from several reporters, one from the *Atlanta Journal and Constitution*, another from CNN, but he doesn't return the calls.

Michaelson is briefly interviewed on the local news.

Taber recognizes the parking lot of the morgue in the background.

"I have no comment," he says, following the advice of their newly hired lawyers, advice delivered by email just hours earlier:

Say absolutely nothing to the press.

On TV Michaelson adds: "When you watch the show—it's called AMERICAN AUTOPSY, Tuesdays at ten on the Science Channel—when you watch it, you'll find that while certainly entertaining, what it's really about is education and, well, humanity. And life. But I have to reiterate, regarding this lawsuit, I have absolutely no comment."

☽

For his own eighteenth birthday his parents gave him a Bible. He's decided to do the same for Katie. At Davis-Kidd bookstore, the Bibles occupy a single shelf at the border between philosophy and Christianity. He'd give her Lizzie's if it weren't lost. He expected it to turn up at some point, but he's begun to wonder if perhaps it disappeared at the hospital, in the disorder of those final weeks.

It takes him a while to find a Bible that devotes more space to scripture than footnotes. As if the bias of translation weren't enough. He doesn't make a habit of reading the Bible, but he'd prefer his religious experiences without the contamination of someone else's ideas. Wouldn't his daughter feel the same? Is she not smart enough to draw her own conclusions? He chooses the New King James Version, the translation his wife preferred. It looks and feels the way a Bible should: leather of deep crimson, pages edged in gold.

He carries it upstairs and pays the cashier. He goes out through the mall, thinking he might find a place to buy a card. A display table has been set up in the thoroughfare outside the bookstore, beyond the view of the cashier. The exposure of the merchandise—all of these books, not even in the store, just waiting to be stolen—elicits in Taber a vague sense of unease. He understands the bookstore's strategy, but feels posters in the window would accomplish the same result.

Tina McGavin stands at the display table. She wears running tights that reveal her trim figure. She must have come here from the gym, perhaps the Green Hills Y just down the street. She puts down a book and thoughtfully backs around the display table. Taber looks for her husband. A lawyer would tell him to walk away, but he can't bring himself to move.

Now she's staring at him across a display of cookbooks and upholstered notepads.

"What do *you* want?" she says.

He nods, unable to speak, and finds himself reaching across the table to shake hands. His hand seems to move on its own, out of reflex, and when they shake, they avoid each other's eyes, glancing in various directions, as if their clasped hands belonged to other people.

Her husband emerges from the restaurant on the opposite side of the thoroughfare. What's his name? Brian? He carries a pair of drinks in foam cups with caps and straws.

"Don't even speak to him," he says, passing one of the drinks to his wife. "He's trash."

Brian. The name for some reason seems to fit. He purses his lips over the straw and glares at Taber, his neck throbbing as he swallows. Tina is drinking as well, and he can actually hear the gulping sounds as they imbibe. Their drinking seems to have an aggressive quality. They stare at him while they do it, as if to say, we'll consume, we'll live, despite what you've done to us.

"We just want to know why," Tina says.

That's not all you want, Taber thinks: you want money, as much as you can squeeze out of us.

"I'm so sorry," he says, shaking his head.

"Is he admitting his guilt?" Brian says with a flash of excitement. He rattles the ice in his cup and slurps the last of his drink.

"A terrible thing happened," Taber says, "but it was an accident. I had nothing to do with that TV show."

"How can you say that?" Tina asks. "You gave us your word he wouldn't be filmed and there he was."

"He's just trying to pass the blame," Brian says.

There's something inauthentic in Brian's display of outrage. It's clear he's angry, as he has every right to be, but Taber has the impression that he doesn't quite know how to manage the hatred he's supposed to feel. The sarcasm and rancor seem like part of an unrehearsed performance. Taber suspects Brian would prefer to mourn in solitude, rather than mold his grief in the service of litigation.

But Tina seems to know exactly what she's doing. Perhaps the lawsuit was her idea. Taber imagines her easily capable of setting aside emotion while enacting a slow, cold vengeance.

He looks at her and says, "Our fellow, Andrea Gill—she's named in the lawsuit. You should know that, of all people, she's least to blame."

Tina raises her eyebrows. "Is she the one with the exercise routine?"

"The swimmer," says Brian, shaking his head in disgust.

"She used Ken as a backdrop," Tina says, "so she could stand there talking about her balanced lifestyle."

Taber can see through the plate glass behind them into a restaurant where an old man sitting alone drops ice cubes into his bowl of steaming soup.

"The TV show notwithstanding," Taber says, "I want you both to know that your son was treated with the utmost respect."

He thinks he sees Brian McGavin roll his eyes, but he can't be sure.

On his way home he considers for the first time how easily he allowed the intrusion of the TV show. Instead of just banning the camera crew from his own autopsies, he should have stopped the show altogether. He should have appealed to the state medical board, even if it meant jeopardizing his friendship with Michaelson, or his position in the group. He can't imagine Michaelson firing him, but it would probably be easier to face joblessness than this lawsuit. While a part of him wants to proclaim his innocence—he has at least one email documenting his objection to the show—there's no ignoring the simple fact that he was the one ultimately responsible for Ken's body.

He pulls into the driveway and parks behind Katie's Honda. There's movement in his rear view mirror, six or seven dogs lurking at the base of his driveway. They slink in and out of the shadows cast by the street-lights, some visible only by the white vapor from their mouths.

Before getting out of his car, he calls Katie and has her turn on the outside lights. He has no good reason for believing the light will offer any kind of protection, but the dogs hardly seem to notice as he hurries to the front door.

He and Katie watch them through the living room window. There is a possum carcass in the gutter, partially concealed by shadow. The dogs keep drawing near it and then pulling away, as if weighing revulsion against hunger.

"There's something I need to talk to you about," he says. "Your friend Ken McGavin—as you know, he was brought to our office after he died."

"You did the autopsy."

"That's right," he says, nodding. "It turns out he appeared—completely by accident—in the background on that TV show." He waits for her to respond, but she says nothing.

"It was just a brief glimpse," he says, "but his parents recognized a tattoo."

"The Road Runner," she says.

He holds back an urge to ask how familiar she'd been with this tattoo on Ken's thigh. Had they reached such intimacy that she actually saw it? Surely he'd only told her about it.

"So what happens now?" she says.

"There's a lawsuit," he says. "I wanted you to hear it from me before you heard it somewhere else. There's already been a story on the news and an article in *The Tennessean*."

"All right," she says.

What does she mean, all right?

"You have every reason to be angry at me," he says.

"Why would I be angry?" she asks.

"I let down your friend," he says. "I didn't mean for him to be shown on TV."

"You shouldn't be so hard on yourself," she says. "If Ken's parents are suing you, it's because they don't know you. They don't realize the kind of person you are."

"Maybe we'll call you as a character witness," he says.

"I'll do it," she says, not realizing he is making a joke, and her misunderstanding evokes such affection that he doesn't have the heart to correct her.

VIII

84

BOTH LAWYERS STAND when Taber enters the conference room. Though a few minutes late, he's the first of his partners to arrive. He knows the older lawyer, Tom Bailey, by reputation. Bailey's family has donated so much money to Vanderbilt that portions of the law school bear his name. It's doubtful he needs whatever income he earns defending physicians. All that sits on the table before him is a blank yellow legal pad. It's his associate, a young woman, who manages the laptop and document case. Taber guesses she's fresh out of law school, making over a hundred thousand dollars a year doing what amounts to secretarial work for Tom Bailey.

While they wait for the other pathologists, Taber reminds Bailey of their mutual acquaintance, Sam Adler, whom Bailey unsuccessfully defended in a malpractice case about ten years ago.

"And how is Sam these days?" Bailey asks.

Taber doesn't mention the lawsuit. It didn't go well for the defense. A surgeon, eager to send home her patient, commandeered an x-ray machine without informing anyone from radiology. She didn't notice the stray guide-wire that had migrated into the patient's heart. The wire was discovered two months later, when the patient nearly died from septic shock. Although Sam Adler never even saw the radiograph, he was named in the lawsuit simply because he happened to be on call that day. The trial dragged on for two years, and the jury ruled against him.

How could Sam Adler be held accountable for a radiograph he never even saw? It would have been a different matter entirely if he'd actually looked at the x-ray and failed to appreciate the significance of the wire. Taber has always suspected some miscalculation on Bailey's part. The outcome seems to prove a flaw in the system or the lawyer, likely both. In either case, Taber can't help but doubt Bailey's prospects against the family of Ken McGavin.

Of all the lawyers in Nashville, why did Michaelson hire Bailey?

The decision likely had more to do with Bailey's social clout than his skill at litigation.

The other pathologists file quietly into the conference room, and Taber holds back his irritation at Tamagi's usual avoidance of handshaking. Without apology or excuse, Tamagi simply pretends not to see Bailey's hand, which hovers for an extended moment of awkwardness until Andrea reaches out and shakes it.

Before sitting back down Bailey takes off his suit jacket and drapes it over the chair beside him. He wears a starched, monogrammed shirt and cufflinks. Taber can make out the golf clubs and tees adorning Bailey's suspenders. Perhaps Bailey and Michaelson play golf together at the Belle Meade Country Club.

"First off," Bailey says, "I have to warn you this isn't going to be an easy road, but from our standpoint, you have good reason to be optimistic, very optimistic."

Taber looks at the younger lawyer. He admires the gentle speed of her fingers on the keyboard as Bailey speaks.

"Without going into too much detail," Bailey says, dabbing his eyes with a wad of tissue, "I can assure you there are several precedents where courts have protected the right of newspapers to display photographs of, how shall we say, human remains. As for the issue of privacy, well, there is great disagreement among jurists as to whether the right to privacy extends beyond death. There are plenty of instances of human remains being displayed to the public. Consider the catacombs of Paris: is one obligated to track down the families of every skeleton on display?"

He turns to his associate, who stops typing and takes a moment to shuffle papers. Taber wonders if the two of them are carrying out some performance, if perhaps she's now expected to recite a monologue on privacy and death.

"The plaintiffs," she says, "are working under the erroneous assumption that Ken McGavin's body is the property of his relatives." She pauses long enough to glance down at her notes. "A man in the 1980's, having murdered his own brother, tried to prevent an autopsy on the grounds that it would constitute an unjust seizure of his property, but the court denied his claims to protection under the Fourth Amendment."

"That's right," Bailey says. "The court is basically saying that relatives have no property right whatsoever when it comes to the body of a loved one."

"That's wonderful!" Landman says. "I mean, it's wonderful for our case, right?"

Taber thinks she should know better. A better lawyer would have an equally convincing case on hand to confute the point.

"What if we just settle?" Taber says.

"Are you insane?" Tamagi says. "Listen to the man—we have a slam-dunk case."

"We showed their son's body on TV without permission," Taber says. "Maybe we should just accept that we made a mistake and pay for it."

"We did nothing wrong," Tamagi says. "If anybody made a mistake, it's the production company. They're responsible for the content of each show."

"They're the ones keeping track of who gives permission," Landman says. "We're just doing our work as usual."

"They're going to claim that consent was the responsibility of the physician," Taber says. "Either way, it's our job to make sure nothing happens to a body while it's here."

"But nothing happened!" Tamagi says, slapping the table. "That's what I don't understand about all this 'abuse of a corpse' business. We treated Ken McGavin like anyone else."

"Clearly there's been no abuse," says Michaelson, who has been surprisingly quiet till now. "That will be immediately obvious to any jury."

Bailey and his associate exchange glances. He raises a hand to his mouth and clears his throat. It seems to Taber a slightly theatrical gesture, but it has the effect of silencing the room.

"All of you make valid points," he says, nodding at Taber.

"I wouldn't call it 'a slam-dunk case,' per se, but our strategy will primarily be to focus blame on the production company." He turns to his associate.

"8th Window Productions," she says.

"We freely admit that a mistake was made," he says, "but the mistake was theirs, not ours."

"Are you representing all five of us?" Taber says. "I mean, what if we disagree on strategy?"

"I need to inform you that we're here to represent the interests of the Forensic Group," Bailey says. "If any of you, as individuals, feel your interests are in conflict with those of the group as a whole, I advise you to obtain separate counsel. You mentioned settling, offering them money to drop the case, and I think it's a valid option, but for now I feel our case is too strong to go down that road."

"Settling would be a waste of money," Tamagi says. "We're all used to the witness stand—we'll hardly need any preparation for it."

"I agree," says Michaelson. "I feel horrible about what the McGavins have gone through, but frankly, we haven't done anything wrong, and I for one have no intention of doling out my hard-earned money to make amends for someone else's mistake. And let me say this—" His hesitation adds weight to his next statement. "I *know* the McGavins. My son and theirs go to the same school. Like I said, I feel horrible about what they've gone through, but in a situation like this, there's no room for emotion."

"There's too much at stake," Landman says.

"The point is," Michaelson says, "Brian McGavin is a nice guy, but—how can I say it—he's *meek*. He isn't a fighter. I just don't think these are the kind of people willing to take the gloves off."

He hears the voice of Brian McGavin: *Don't even speak to him, he's trash.* Is this the language of the meek? And what about Tina? Taber's convinced she's the sort to take off the gloves.

"It's good to know your enemy," Bailey says.

Andrea sits on the far side of Tamagi. As usual in group meetings, she hasn't said a word, but of the five physicians at the table, she's the one most in need of her own lawyer. None of the others appeared on television with Ken McGavin's body. It's only a matter of time before Tamagi and Landman, and perhaps Michaelson as well, start diverting blame. He knows what they'll say: she should have noticed the tattoo, she should have covered it. It won't matter that the details of cadaver apparel lie far outside her job description.

¶

Memos from Foreman & Sparks warn against discussing any aspect of the McGavin case with the press. So Michaelson's announcement, inviting everyone to be sure to watch *Backtalk with Barbara Brown*, comes as a surprise, not just to his partners, but also to Tom Bailey, who sends the entire group an email, all but accusing them of outright stupidity. For Michaelson, it seems, the benefits of publicity outweigh the risk of legal damage.

As it happens, his appearance on *Backtalk* has nothing to do with the lawsuit. He's been invited for expert commentary on the death of a singer who inadvertently strangled himself while masturbating. A review article in the *American Journal of Forensic Pathology*, published in the late nineties, established Michaelson as an authority on the phenomenon of erotic self-asphyxiation. The singer is relatively unknown, but Barbara Brown portrays sexual strangulation as a growing trend among the celebrity elite.

Michaelson isn't physically present on *BACKTALK*: he speaks to Babs and her audience from a video-screen over the stage. He wears a white coat and tie. If not for the slather of make-up and eye-liner, a viewer might think the camera crew had caught him during a busy day of doctoring. He doesn't seem surprised when she brings up the lawsuit.

"I understand you're having legal troubles of your own," she says.

"Out of respect for the family in question, I'd prefer not to say anything—except that I'm confident this misunderstanding will soon be worked out to the satisfaction of everyone involved."

"You're referring to the individuals who recognized the body of their 17-year-old son on your show, *AMERICAN AUTOPSY*."

"I can't comment, except to say we've done everything possible to present our patients with dignity and compassion, and we've made every effort to conceal their identities. The primary purpose of *AMERICAN AUTOPSY*, from my standpoint, is education. Education and authenticity."

"You're showing real autopsies, in a real morgue." Babs gives an exaggerated shiver.

"That's right," he says. "What the show does, really, is give an honest portrayal of our work in the morgue, and how we, as forensic pathologists, contribute to investigations of death—murder or otherwise."

"In general, when it comes to forensic medicine, do you feel like the public is misinformed?"

"Absolutely, no question, which is why there's such a need for a TV show like *AMERICAN AUTOPSY*. There's always going to be controversy when you're perceived to be pushing the envelope."

"That's what you're doing? Pushing the envelope? If it hadn't been this lawsuit, this particular family, do you think it would have been someone else?"

"I don't know," he says. "I guess we always figured there would be controversy in one form or another."

"I'll tell you how we deal with controversy here on *Backtalk*," she says, drawing a murmur of excitement from her mostly female audience. "We decide for ourselves!"

The audience roars, and she says it again, even louder this time, and Michaelson smiles and politely claps, seemingly confused by the applause. They clearly aren't shouting for *American Autopsy*. It seems that on *Backtalk*, this phrase, "We decide for ourselves," has implications understood only by longtime viewers.

IX

KATIE HAS SOMETHING on her mind, Taber can tell. She's hardly touched her dinner, even though it's her birthday and Café Nona is her favorite restaurant.

"When you do an autopsy on someone with mental illness," she asks, "can you actually *see* an abnormality?"

"Good question," he says.

She looks away, obviously annoyed—either by his empty compliment or his tendency to address her like a student.

"There are many types of mental illness," he says, "some associated with systemic disease—"

"A person with depression," she says, rolling her eyes but doing it somehow with her entire upper body.

"All right," he says. "What exactly are you asking?"

"I always hear how depression is really just a physical illness."

"That's true," he says. "It's thought to involve neurotransmitters in certain parts of the brain, but that's probably just part of the picture."

"But it's not something you can see in a microscope."

"Generally no," he says, not sure where she's going.

"If there's a difference," she says, "why can't you see it when you use those stains that target specific chemicals?"

This time he really does think it's a good question, but he refrains from saying so.

"As far as I know," he says, "we don't yet have the ability to distinguish a depressed brain from normal. The difference is just too subtle—but a lot of interesting work is being done in the field of molecular imaging."

"You asked if Ken was a happy person," she says. "I told you he was, but I could have been wrong about him."

Taber's first thought is that someone at school found a suicide note.

"Did you hear something?" he asks.

She nods. "Supposedly he had these 'dark spells,' where he'd just, like, withdraw into himself for days on end."

"Who told you that?"

"A reliable source," she says, needlessly cryptic, and then adds, "Guys on the wrestling team."

"Tell me more."

"The night of the homecoming dance—when he didn't show up, I guess some of his friends went to his house and found him sitting in his car in the garage."

"Was the engine running?"

"No," she says. "They said no."

Taber stares at his daughter. Nothing so obvious as a note, but it does raise the question of depression, which in turn supports the argument of suicide. What she's telling him amounts to little more than hearsay. It certainly doesn't carry enough weight for him to addend the report, which for all intents and purposes he can't even consider now that he's being sued by the victim's parents.

"Sometimes it's better to let sleeping dogs—" He stops short, knowing how she hates clichés.

"What about that little thing called the truth?"

He's touched by her innocence—that for all her dark posturing, she still clings to the idea of the truth being always knowable.

"Of course I want to know what really happened," he says. "But that's not always possible."

He pokes at his noodles, finds a cube of chicken. He's aware of her waiting. Her silence seems to demand an answer: *Did Ken McGavin kill himself or not?* Perhaps he did, but what good would it do her to believe it?

"I'm certain it was an accident," he says, "even in light of these dark spells or whatever you want to call them."

The waiter, following Taber's private instructions, brings a slice of chocolate cake with a single candle but refrains from any further display such as singing, because that would cause Katie undue embarrassment. She upends the candle and stubs out the flame on the plate. Taber eats the larger share, leaving the last bite for her.

Her present is still in the sack from the bookstore. He should have had it wrapped, but she doesn't seem to mind. He wonders if she even remembers the artistry and care with which her mother used to wrap gifts. She flips through the pages of the New King James and says it's just what she wanted.

¶

He takes Ellington Parkway downtown and parks in a public deck near Printer's Alley. An elevator that smells like urine carries him down to the damp sidewalk. On the ground behind a dumpster lies a tangled garment. He bends for a closer look but refrains from touching what turns out to be a woman's bra, the lace pattern still visible under a coating of filth. He remembers the mile-long chain of bras hanging from telephone poles for breast cancer awareness. What happened to all of them? Perhaps one of them found its way here. He imagines it skittering on the pavement, a kind of urban tumbleweed.

The offices of Cantrel, Barry & Pietch are located in one of the older buildings close to the river. A hand-written sign in the wood-paneled lobby tells him the elevator's out of order, so he climbs the stairs to the fourth floor. The receptionist escorts him back to a conference room where Jason Gardner sits with a laptop.

"You're right to get your own lawyer," Gardner says, pouring him a glass of water.

Taber first encountered Jason Gardner a few years ago, in a trial on negligent homicide: a baby experienced a long, painful death from bowel obstruction while her mother enjoyed a heroin binge next door. Taber remembers Gardner's maddening ability to conjure, as though from vapor, such details as to give an impression of controversy where none existed. After the acquittal of that mother, even the prosecutor had to acknowledge Gardner's genius. But Taber has another, simpler reason for choosing him: he's new to private practice, and therefore more affordable than most attorneys.

"I have emails proving that I was opposed to the TV show from the start," Taber says. "And anyone on the staff will testify that I barred TV cameras from my autopsies."

"That would certainly help if it weren't your signature on Ken McGavin's autopsy report."

Gardner slides three stapled packets across the table—copies of briefs from the lawyers for the plaintiffs and two defendants, 8th Window Productions and the pathologists.

"The Forensic Group's lawyers are asserting a first amendment right to broadcast images of bodies," Gardner says.

"They're making it an issue of free speech."

"The court has held that free speech is protected when the facts are truthful, newsworthy, and in the public interest."

"Murder and suicide are certainly newsworthy," Taber says.

"And you can't say the autopsies aren't truthful."

"The plaintiffs are accusing you of violating their privacy," Gardner says. "The defense—for both the Forensic Group and the production company—have countered that the right to privacy ends with death, and there are precedents to support that argument."

Taber nods. He's been through this line of reasoning with the other lawyers.

"The supreme court has traditionally handled free speech questions on a case by case basis," Gardner says. "It has refused to place a general ban on truthful publication. The brief from the

Forensic Group mentions several cases, namely *Smith v. Daily Mail Publishing*, in which the court upholds a publisher's right to release information normally withheld from the public."

"Like an autopsy," Taber says. "The autopsy report is admissible in court but never disclosed to the public."

"The counter-argument is that private tragedy isn't newsworthy. There was a case in Chicago in 1996, *Green v. the Chicago Tribune*, where a dying gang-member was photographed in a hospital room with his mother. Gang violence was all over the news at that time, but when the kid's mother sued, the court ruled that those private photographs weren't newsworthy."

"But how often is death not a private tragedy? Even when we can't find anything close to a next-of-kin, I suspect that, if you looked hard enough, there'd be someone, somewhere, saddened by the loss," Taber says. "By the logic of the case from Chicago, very few, if any, deaths would qualify as newsworthy."

"The death itself might be newsworthy, but not a photograph of the body."

"I guess it all depends on whether or not the family gives permission."

"On some level that's true, but even when you have a family's permission, you're still susceptible to this charge of—"He reads, "'Interference with or mishandling of human remains.'"

"Abusing a corpse." Taber cringes while uttering the very phrase.

"In 2003, when a photojournalist in Ohio took pictures of a cadaver, the court ruled that his photographs constituted a form of abuse."

"But the group's lawyers gave an impression that there were precedents for cases very similar to ours, where newspapers or magazines were allowed to display pictures of cadavers. If you look at any newspaper, the *New York Times* or whatever, it seems like they show pictures of the dead and wounded every time there's a bomb attack in Afghanistan or Iraq. I remember pictures of Saddam Hussein's dead sons all over the media."

"The Forensic Group's lawyers are touting a case from 1956, *Bremmer v. Journal-Tribune Publishing Company*, where the court upheld a newspaper's right to run a photograph of a dead child. The problem with that case is that the child was photographed in a public place."

"Like a battlefield," Taber says.

"Exactly," he says. "The plaintiffs don't quite acknowledge that a corpse can be photographed in a public place, but they do make the argument that the morgue should be protected by law as a place of seclusion."

"That explains the charges related to privacy. How did they say it?"

"'Invasion of privacy based on intrusion upon seclusion,'" he says. "The other is, 'Invasion of privacy for publicizing private facts.'"

"Right, and what about this idea of abuse?"

Gardner folds his hands over his papers and looks at Taber. "If a photographer manipulates a corpse to enhance the image, then he's committing an abuse."

"As far as I know, no cadaver was ever—manipulated," Taber says.

"It doesn't have to be as brazen as posing a body for dramatic effect. Your *New York Times* photographer, for instance—if he were to clear debris off the body, or set up some prop beside it—you could make an argument for abuse."

"Hold on," Taber says. "The argument is moot in the case of Ken McGavin, right? Filming it was a complete accident. We couldn't have used it as a—prop or whatever—if we never intended to film it in the first place."

"The fact that it was onscreen at all indicates that you intended it to be there. We might have argued otherwise if it had shown up in the background during one of the autopsies, but in the context of an interview, it looks like a planned backdrop. Either while filming or in the editing room, whatever, someone made a decision to display that body and tattoo. That interview could have taken place in a hallway, but somebody liked the dramatic effect of a body in the background."

Dramatic effect. He remembers the hollow clink of a bullet in a metal bowl.

"The Forensic Group's lawyers have produced heaps of documents to support their claim that the right to privacy ends with death, but they've completely disregarded a fundamental issue." He pauses to fill his and Taber's water glasses. "It's not the privacy of Ken McGavin we should be worried about," he says. "It's the privacy of his parents."

"What if he had no living relatives?" Taber says. "What if it was a friend, an acquaintance, who had recognized the tattoo on TV?"

"I doubt they'd have been offended to the point of suing, but like you said, it's almost always a private tragedy for someone, somewhere. The courts routinely prohibit the release of autopsy photographs in celebrity cases. John F. Kennedy's autopsy pictures were sealed, in part out of respect for the privacy of his family."

"If someone had illegally published a photograph of JFK's body, would that person have been prosecuted?"

"They could have been sued by surviving family members. The point is, the morgue is a place where people have a reasonable expectation of seclusion. Like a hospital, or a bedroom, it's a place where the law theoretically protects one from public exposure. In *Douglas v. Stokes*, the Kentucky Court of Appeals wrote—" He turns the page and reads, "'If the defendant had wrongfully taken possession of the nude body of the plaintiff's dead child and exposed it to public view—it would not be doubted that an injury was done. When he wrongfully used a photograph of it, a like wrong was done.'"

"That's going a little far," Taber says.

"What can I tell you? This is the kind of thing juries love."

From downtown he takes Broadway home. The sun is going down, and tourists already crowd the sidewalk. Standing out among the neon signs and honky-tonks is a single dilapidated storefront with plywood windows. Over the padlocked door a faded and barely legible sign reads "McDuff's". The former Irish pub closed about eight years ago, not long after the owner and his wife were gunned down by teenagers in the shaded entryway now occupied by a ragged guitarist strumming for pocket change. The owner of the pub survived, but not his wife. Taber performed the autopsy. The abandoned building saddens him whenever he passes it—something about the owner's refusal to sell or renovate, the obvious expense, as if the dilapidation itself had become a kind of memorial.

X

HE SITS WITH HIS BACK TO THE DOOR—a ready escape should he change his mind about the settlement. The McGavins seem to have lost weight since he last saw them. Tina stares out the window, which offers a view of the Cumberland River. Brian drums his fingertips against the polished surface of the conference table, his eyes scanning the shelves of legal volumes as if searching for a particular title.

It's Gardner's first encounter with Mike Daniels, the McGavins' lawyer, but while waiting for the mediator they bond over their shared disdain for the overabundance of tattoos in professional basketball.

"They're all marching to the same beat," Gardner says, but off Daniels' blank look has to explain that the word *tattoo* also refers to a military drumbeat.

Taber as well missed the joke, but still sees it as a point of pride that the opposing lawyer can't keep up with Gardner's sense of humor. It would be an auspicious sign if they were going to trial, but no one expects a battle of wits, just a brief negotiation in an informal setting. The relaxed atmosphere might explain, at least in part, why neither attorney seems to have considered the potential awkwardness around the subject of tattoos. Tina's eyes are fixed on a painted landscape, and Taber wonders if what she sees there is her son's Road Runner.

In comes the hunched figure of Roland Kitt, the official mediator. He sets aside his bird-head cane and checks his gold pocket watch. He apologizes for being late but instead of offering an excuse merely pants for breath. The retired judge looks for a moment like he might be having a heart attack, but Taber finds reassurance in the strength of his handshake, a healthy flow of blood warming the skin.

After the introductions, when they've taken their seats around the table, Daniels says, "My clients' decision to accept this meeting in no way reflects a lack of confidence in their case."

"Likewise," Gardner says, "my client is seeking mediation for the sole purpose of avoiding the strain of a prolonged trial."

Daniels slides a legal pad to Gardner, a number scrawled at the top of the page:

500

Five hundred thousand dollars, far more than Taber expected. It seems like an arbitrary number, not calculated so much as whimsically suggested by Daniels. Gardner writes 200 in the space below.

"You've got to be kidding me," Tina says.

Daniels writes another number. "This is as low as we're willing to go."

Four hundred thousand dollars. Gardner tries three hundred, but Daniels refuses even to look at the page.

"As low as we're willing to go," he says again.

"Let's not be unreasonable," Gardner says.

Daniels glances at Tina, who eyes the notepad and shakes her head.

"Then I guess we're done here," Daniels says, sliding back his chair.

"We'll accept this," Taber says, "under the condition that Andrea Gill be removed from the lawsuit."

"The trainee in the Forensic Group," Gardner explains.

"Dr. Andrea Gill."

"Absolutely not," Tina says, a kind of wildness in her bloodshot eyes. She turns to the mediator and says, "He's probably sleeping with her."

"Even if that were true—" Gardner begins.

"To reach an agreement," says Kitt, "each party has to be willing to make concessions."

Tina's phone rings and she silences it without looking at the name of the caller. Taber glimpses the background photograph, their son kneeling beside a golden retriever.

"Your dog," Taber says. "Did you ever find it?"

A moment's hesitation and she nods and says, "Thank you."

"Turns out he was never lost," Brian says. "Just roaming the neighborhood."

She cuts him an irritated glance. A man incapable of deception, but the first mistake was hers: she shouldn't have mentioned the dog that day at the morgue.

"Could I have a moment with my lawyer?" Taber asks.

"I think we could all use a break," Kitt says.

In an empty office across the hall Taber says, "I did them a favor by calling their son's death an accident."

"You certainly can't expect gratitude," Gardner says, all but laughing. "Besides, you'd completely undermine any argument of professional competence by admitting you were in the habit of doing favors."

"They know he committed suicide," he says in a tone of shock, as if their deception were an outrage on the level of abusing a corpse. Gardner shakes his head. "If you issued an addendum, it would be seen as retaliatory."

"Not an addendum—a second opinion."

Gardner looks at him. "You could submit the case to another pathologist?"

"Why not?" He shrugs. "I'd have been justified in recusing myself at the outset. The question is, how far are the McGavins willing to go to keep their son's death from being called a suicide?"

"That's harsh," says Gardner, but he clearly appreciates the strategy of using the manner of death as leverage.

"Whatever it takes to get her dropped from the lawsuit."

"If they bite, we could probably bring down the dollar amount as well."

Taber shakes his head. "Let's just stick with the four hundred."

"You sure?" Gardner asks, but Taber can tell he understands. It's a morally dubious tactic, not to mention a cruelty against these people who have lost their only child, but Taber can at least comfort himself with the knowledge that he isn't doing it for money.

Back in the conference room Gardner comes straight to the point: "The tragic loss of your son was officially designated an accident, but Dr. Taber, given the potential for bias, would be justified in submitting the case for an outside opinion."

Brian looks away but Tina stares impassively at Taber. He wills himself to hold eye contact even as he retreats into a memory from childhood—or a *feeling* from childhood—when all mythologies pointed to a reality beyond the world he could perceive with his senses. He had a powerful conviction of himself as an outsider even in his own home—a visitor from a place he couldn't quite remember. That feeling of dislocation must have ebbed over time without his even noticing. And now, for the first time, he realizes he lost something essential.

"We'll give you the girl," Tina says.

¶

The settlement: four hundred thousand dollars, to be paid in monthly installments over a period of six years. And Andrea's name will be removed from the suit.

He's certain he could have found a worthier cause on which to spend Lizzie's life insurance. He does her no honor by using it as penance for AMERICAN AUTOPSY, a show whose very existence he opposed. Considering the cost of tuition at Princeton, he expects he'll also have to sell the house and move into an apartment.

His partners don't seem to notice the coincidence of his settlement and Andrea's release from the lawsuit. He's obligated to keep the exact cost to himself, which is just as well since he's somewhat embarrassed to have paid so much. But when none of the others ask him the amount, he worries they might already know. Perhaps their lawyers learned through back channels.

Hiring a separate lawyer has made him somewhat of an outcast among his partners. They seem to be under the impression that his abandonment will leave them each responsible for a greater share of the legal fees. Weeks pass before he even realizes Tamagi and Landman aren't speaking to him, their version of the silent treatment being hardly distinguishable from their usual avoidance of social interaction.

Their impending divorce is the talk of the office, though no surprise after their televised insults. For Taber the demise of their marriage offers a glimmer of hope: one of them will almost certainly need to find a new job. Preferably Tamagi, but either way, Michaelson will have no choice but to hire a replacement. And of course there's no better candidate than Andrea.

When he mentions it, Michaelson nods and says, "We'll see."

"She won't have a problem getting hired somewhere else," Taber says.

He's standing in the doorway of Michaelson's office, not sure if he should enter. A month ago, and for almost fifteen years before that, he would have crossed the threshold without a second thought.

"Vanderbilt would kill to have her back," Taber says.

"We need to wait for the dust to settle," Michaelson says, not looking up from his computer.

Yesterday's *Tennessean* sits on Michaelson's desk. An editorial portrays him as a kind of dandified sociopath, more interested in fame than medicine. Michaelson seems to have been reading it, or re-reading it, when Taber knocked.

"That was a hatchet job," Taber says. He crosses the office and drops the newspaper in the trashcan.

"Whatever," Michaelson says, "it is what it is."

This bland affability, speaking without saying anything, seems to be Michaelson's way of expressing his sense of betrayal. It's more off-putting, perhaps, than Tamagi and Landman's refusal to speak to him at all.

"No one of consequence still reads *THE TENNESSEAN*," Taber says.

"I read it," Michaelson says. "You do, too."

Michaelson's newest desk ornament is a human skull. Taber can't resist picking it up for a closer look. He spots a crack in the dome, so subtle he has to hold it to the light to be sure.

Trauma, he thinks. Or maybe someone dropped it.

XI

RAIN POUNDS against the skylights of the autopsy suite. It's Saturday and he and Chaquita have only one case: a 54-year-old mechanic found by his roommate. Renalda's photographs show him slouched on a sofa, as if he'd died watching television. A half-eaten cheeseburger sits on the coffee table, but Renalda doesn't know whether it belongs to the victim or his roommate.

The organs look like specimens in an anatomy textbook. Try as he might, he's unable to find a cause of death. Not even a trace of atherosclerosis in the coronary arteries. If the toxicology studies come back negative, he'll have to accept that the truth has eluded him.

Cause of death: unknown. At least to him. He has a case like this every couple of months. They invariably leave him with doubts. Has he missed something? Every autopsy is a problem with a solution: would a better pathologist have figured it out? Such cases nurture his secret conviction that there are ways of dying not yet known by science.

He's of no more use than the well-meaning friend who says, "It was just his time." When death comes for no discernible reason, there is a tendency to make one up: he offended the gods, he was never quite right in the head, he ate too many cheeseburgers.

After the autopsy Chaquita hastens to clean up and prepare the body for transport to the funeral home. She clearly doesn't want to be here—she's worried about the rain. Her growing distress obliges Taber to lift his usual ban on internet use in the autopsy suite. He stands behind her as she pulls up images of overflowing creeks and flooded bridges. There is standstill traffic on I-24. Could there be flooding on the highway as well?

Chaquita's worries might be warranted after all. He wonders how long it will take him to get home. He remembers his four-hour commute after the snowstorm in 2003. He'd rather wait out the rain and draft his autopsy report than waste time in traffic.

He stops in the break room on his way back to his office. The TV shows helicopter footage of a pair of horses standing knee-deep in a flooded pasture. The voice-over mentions Antioch, where Chaquita lives. Out the window, he watches her leap over a frothing gutter and sprint to her car.

He calls and leaves Katie a message telling her to stay inside. He thinks about the Adlers across the street—their perennial problem with basement flooding.

Rain battering the window of his office, he sits at his microscope with a stack of slides, but he can't take his attention from the local news on his desktop computer. Some kind of free-floating warehouse knocks aside cars on I-24. The width of two lanes and the length of a semi, this juggernaut heaves past vehicles sunk up to their roofs and turned at various angles in the current. Printed on its side is the word HOPE. When it stalls against the back end of an SUV, Taber notices the mud brown water ripping past it.

The power goes out and he sits in darkness listening to the rain on the roof, a steady roar on tapping tin. He wasn't aware of the sound till the lights went out.

His phone trills on his desk.

"The driveway's covered in water," Katie says.

"What about the garage?"

"Still dry."

He thinks of the empty creek bed in the back yard—if that shallow, grass-lined impression could even be called a creek bed—and all the junk he has stored in the garage: his mother's furniture, boxes of papers and books. Old autopsy reports.

"Go into the garage," he says. "If there's anything there you want to keep, you better move it inside."

"Already done," she says. "My bike's in the kitchen."

How much higher will the water rise? It never occurred to him to purchase flood insurance. Not only will he have to sell the house in a bottom market, but with water damage as well. At least he doesn't have a basement.

He has yet to tell Katie of his plan to sell the house where she grew up. When the time comes, he'll say it's too large, that he can't stand living in it by himself. He's already met with a real estate agent. He figures he'll move into an apartment or condominium, perhaps one of the innumerable loft-style units sitting empty in downtown Nashville. He's heard about condos in the Gulch selling at auction for half their original price, even less.

When the generators come on, he notices a stain on the carpet of his office—a leak of some kind, but not from the ceiling. He slides out one of the bookcases and peers behind it. The water stain seems darkest along the baseboard. Perhaps it's coming from Michaelson's office next door. He picks up papers and books, places the trashcan and hard-drive on his desk.

His feet make squelching sounds on the carpet of Michaelson's office. He lifts the hard-drive onto the desk. He unplugs the microscope and computer, and takes the books off the bottom shelves. He does the same in Tamagi and Landman's offices, and in the scene investigators' cubicles. He clears their trashcans, shredders, hard-drives, backpacks, magazines, and photo albums off the damp floors.

Papers are scattered on Andrea's desk, mostly journal articles. He recognizes a print-out of one of his own: "*Thanatophilus* insect succession in decomposing human skeletal muscle in moist environments." He runs his fingers over the notes she's jotted on the taxonomy of beetles. By touching what she's written, he imagines somehow making contact with her pen and the fingers that held it.

Would she ever consider him? She's 33, thirteen years his junior, but perhaps the medical hierarchy has fixed an even greater distance between them. Perhaps she'll always see him in that sterile way he viewed his own attendings during residency and fellowship. But now that she's signed a contract to join the group—Michaelson finally made her an offer—they'll be working together as equals in a matter of months.

He could suggest a drink after work and, if that went well, an actual date where he took her to dinner and perhaps afterward kissed her or spent the night. Would they keep their relationship from their colleagues or come clean? How long before they met each other's families? She'd work to befriend Katie, who in the beginning would resist the idea of her father dating someone. Perhaps, eventually, he'd propose marriage. The second time for them both, there would be a simple ceremony of just family and perhaps a few close friends.

He's been tempted to tell her why the McGavins released her from the lawsuit, but he doubts she'd take kindly to the idea of a secret settlement on her behalf. She'd likely envision some kind of paternalistic negotiation—older men deciding her fate over a handshake. She'd wonder if he expected something in return. Even if he made every effort to convince her otherwise, she'd probably avoid any sort of romantic involvement with him for the very reason that it might be perceived as obligation.

Just by looking, he might not have noticed the shallow water in the autopsy suite. His shoes splash at the border of carpet and linoleum. Ripples lap against the stainless steel legs of the basins.

A gurney holds the body bag from the case he finished before Chaquita left. It seems the weather, not surprisingly, has prevented the mortuary from retrieving the body. Chaquita shouldn't have left it sitting in the autopsy suite. She should have stowed it in a freezer before leaving.

Cause of death: unknown.

There were faint smudges on the hands and fingers. The man worked as an auto mechanic. Why do these details all of a sudden seem relevant to the case? He puts on a pair of gloves.

The water has risen just higher than the rubber soles of his tennis shoes. He feels it soaking through his socks.

He unzips the body bag, exposing the pale skin of the torso. He lifts one of the hands and looks again at the grease stains, easily distinguishable from the ink used for fingerprinting.

What did he miss? The lab will test for poisons—alkaloids, heavy metals, opiates, cyanide, and whatever else. He's considered vasospasm due to cocaine. What about antifreeze? One of the few toxins he can identify without mass spectrometry or gas chromatography.

He searches a panel of cabinets until he finds what he's looking for—a Wood's lamp. The group keeps one on hand for this very purpose, though it's been years since he last used it. He hasn't seen an actual case of ethylene glycol toxicity since medical school.

The skin of the cadaver, in response to ultraviolet light, seems to emit a kind of glow, so faint he doesn't trust that it's real. He turns off the overhead light and again shines the lamp over the body. He illuminates his own skin for comparison. Surely he's imagining it, seeing what he wants to see. The only way to know for certain is to examine the urine.

When he turns the light back on, he sees that the water has risen to his shoelaces.

He carries the Wood's lamp into the vestibule leading to the garage, where the man's fluid and tissue samples await transport to the laboratory. The lock-boxes, against regulation, are all unlocked—yet another uncharacteristic oversight on Chaquita's part—but he's glad not to have search out the keys. He sorts through the contents of one lock-box, then the next, until he finds the hundred-milliliter canister he partially filled with urine two hours earlier.

The Wood's lamp elicits from the urine a vibrant, purple luminescence.

He stands there turning the vial under the lamp, savoring the thrill of diagnosis, its shades of pride and relief. More than anything, he wishes Andrea could be here to see the glowing urine. She probably knows more than he does about fluorescein, the incandescent substance that helps mechanics find coolant leaks. But has she ever seen a case of it firsthand? He pours a small sample of urine into a test-tube to show her on Monday. The lab can spare a few drops for the sake of medical education.

The generator gives out, so he retrieves a flashlight from his office, his shoes splinking in the carpet puddles.

Again he shines his beam over the body bag.

Antifreeze. Supposedly, it has a sweet, fruity taste.

The water on that side of the room has risen above the wheels of the gurney. He needs to secure the body in a freezer. The funeral home won't be collecting it, not today at least—maybe not tomorrow either.

A second light shudders over the faucets and basins. Taber has to shield his eyes against the glare of a flashlight coming down the hallway. Who else would be here on a Saturday evening, during what's looking to be the worst storm Nashville has seen in years? Implausible scenarios flash through his mind—thieves, necrophiliacs, a murderer searching for the body of his victim—in the moments before the flashlight turns on its carrier. The upward shadows cast Michaelson's face in a mask of cartoonish malevolence.

"I saw our building on the news," he says, shining his light over the autopsy suite. "An hour ago, the water was halfway across the parking lot."

"It took you an hour to get here?" he says. "Is that fast or slow?"

"I had to leave my car on Douglas Avenue," he says.

Taber follows him into his office.

"At least one person has died so far," he says, taking off his soaked poncho and the backpack underneath. "A 21-year-old swept away while leaving work, but there's no way the body's coming here."

In the backpack is a plastic garbage bag protecting a camcorder.

"We have to get as much footage as possible," he says as he points the camera at Taber.

"For what, *AMERICAN AUTOPSY*?" Taber can't keep the sarcasm out of his voice.

Michaelson lowers the camera and shrugs. "For documentation," he says.

Documentation. Is this why Michaelson left his family at home, with a sump pump in the basement, and braved the flooding streets of Nashville?

When they return to the autopsy suite, the clear water has risen above their ankles. Taber detects the odor of bleach, combined with the distant foulness of human decomposition.

Michaelson narrates for his imagined audience: "Here we are in the Davidson County morgue, during what might be described as Nashville's Katrina."

Taber puts on a fresh pair of gloves and trundles the gurney into the body storage chamber.

Michaelson says, "Dr. Taber is doing what he can to protect one of his patients."

They stand before a panel of stainless-steel doors, each leading to a refrigerated, hermetically-sealed compartment. At least two of the smaller freezers hold brains, but the larger units, if he remembers correctly, should all be empty. He hates to accelerate decomposition by needlessly opening random freezer doors, but without power, there's no way to check the electronic logs. The first freezer he tries contains a body, but the next is empty, so he slides out its seven-foot tray.

"I need your help," he says.

"Give me a minute," Michaelson says, and treads back into the autopsy suite.

Taber closes the freezer, irritated by Michaelson's failure to appreciate the need for temperature conservation. Michaelson returns with a handful of rubber gloves. He spreads the gloves on the small counter, creating a clean surface for his camcorder and flashlight, both of which he aims at the panel of freezers.

"All right," he says, after adjusting the settings on his camera.

They lift the heavy body bag from the gurney onto the tray. It occurs to Taber that their gloves aren't enough—they probably should have put on protective gowns as well.

As they pass back through the autopsy suite, Taber shines his flashlight into the bone room. The domain of a forensic anthropologist out of Knoxville, who only works here one or two days a week, the bone room is little more than a closet, a narrow passage with shelves of stainless steel against one of the walls. Bone fragments lie on each shelf, arranged into partial skeletons—some near complete, others hardly recognizable as human. The water has climbed to the edge of the bottom shelf, which holds the skeletal remains of two small children and an infant.

Taber squats before the shelves, holding his flashlight in his mouth. He looks at the crowded array of bones, trying to figure out the best way of clearing the bottom shelf without irreparably muddling the anthropologist's efforts at reconstruction.

The infant's bones, whiter than the rest, must have spent time in the sun.

Michaelson turns off his camcorder and sticks it in his pocket.

"So how much did you settle for?" he says.

Taber keeps his eyes fixed on the tiny skull in the beam of his flashlight. He removes the flashlight from his mouth, but hesitates to speak.

"You know I can't answer that."

"Come on," Michaelson says.

Why would he wait till now to bring up the settlement? Did it just happen to enter his mind, or was he waiting for the right moment, hoping to catch Taber off guard?

Michaelson's question answers one of Taber's own: the McGavins' lawyers haven't revealed the amount, as Taber thought they might. No doubt they're hoping to win even more from Michaelson and the others.

"It's enough that I'll have to sell the house," Taber says.

Their flashlights are both pointed at the shelves of bones, but Taber can see Michaelson shaking his head.

"I'm sorry to hear that," Michaelson says.

Is this sarcasm? Is this Michaelson's way of pointing out the foolishness of Taber's decision? If Taber had cast his lot with the group, he'd still be meeting with lawyers on a weekly basis. He'd still be waiting for a trial that may or may not ever come.

"Let's take care of these bones," Taber says, picking up the skull of the infant.

"Hold on," Michaelson says, stepping through the door.

While Michaelson splashes through the autopsy suite, Taber squats before the shelves of bones and considers the water, now above his ankles and drenching the cuffs of his blue jeans. Why didn't he roll up his pant legs?

Michaelson returns to the bone room with a box of plastic ziplock bags reading BIOHAZARD.

"Good idea," Taber says.

He takes one of the bags and gently places the infant's skull inside. He adds the bones of its arms and legs, along with the few ribs and vertebrae. There are no hands or feet. Michaelson has managed to fit the largest of the other two children into its own plastic bag, though the single femur, even at a diagonal, juts higher than the opening. They prop the bags of bones between the legs of the adult on the next highest shelf, well above the water. Taber holds open the third bag, while Michaelson fills it with the last child's bones. This skeleton is more complete than the others, and the smaller bones rattle at the bottom like pebbles.

As they plod back through the autopsy suite, Taber notices a beetle, *coleoptera*, floating lifeless in the clear water.

¶

Three days later he's sitting in his office. The building is near empty, the wet hallways crammed with ventilation pipes and cleaning equipment. Most of the staff are home dealing with property damage. Chaquita has suffered the worst—she lost her entire house.

The bodies of Nashville have been diverted to surrounding counties. He reads of the known flood victims in *THE TENNESSEAN*: a pair of teenagers who tried to run the Harpeth on inner tubes, an elderly couple swept away in their car, a 21-year-old caught walking home from work, a man and his 15-year-old daughter washed from a trailer park.

Since Taber was on call when they died, he feels a certain responsibility for their autopsies. He should be working—not reading the newspaper. He's called the nearest morgues, but they don't need his help. Is this the default mode of rival pathologists, or is it possible that the surrounding counties can so easily absorb the Nashville dead? Perhaps he should drive to Williamson County and insist on doing an autopsy.

The Forensic Group won't be accepting bodies for at least another day. All they've received since the flood is a child's skull, jawless and bare, hand-delivered by the same policeman who discovered it in a pile of roadside debris. It could be ten, fifty, or even a hundred years old, perhaps lifted by water from a shallow grave. Carbon dating might determine the age, but Taber doesn't expect to learn anything more. Renalda spent the morning scouring the area for additional bones. None of the local cemeteries have reported unearthed graves.

An email arrives from Michaelson. "Take Two", reads the subject line.

The message includes a link to the second episode of *American Autopsy* on YouTube.

"Our great-grandchildren will be able to see this," Michaelson writes. "This is where future historians will look when they want to learn about forensics in the twenty-first century."

Surely online availability would prevent the episode from ever airing on television, but he doesn't have the heart to disabuse Michaelson of his apparent conviction that YouTube represents a form of eternal life. When the controversy fades, the first episode might appear online as well—perhaps an edited version, without Ken McGavin.

Taber learned just this morning that the Forensic Group and 8th Window Productions are settling with the McGavins for an undisclosed amount—at least a million dollars, according to Gardner. Part of it will likely come from the company coffers. His own settlement with the McGavins in theory should free him from his partners' debt, but he'd be a fool to count on the usual reimbursements or the annual bonus, though this is the year he needs it most.

In order to view what YouTube deems inappropriate for minors, he has to establish a username and password and affirm that he's over eighteen. As the episode begins to play—the familiar music and credits—his eye is drawn to a thumb-nail image on the right side of his screen: an image of Andrea's face. He clicks on the link, interrupting the second episode midway through the opening credits.

The words AMERICAN AUTOPSY REMIX crawl across a blood-red background.

Autopsy footage flashes on the screen: rapid, jerking movements of scalpels. Latex gloves plunging in and out of an abdominal cavity like the leathery heads of vultures. All of it accompanied by Beethoven's "Ode to Joy".

It takes him a moment to realize that the footage is playing in reverse. Hands sculpt organs on the cutting board. Knives drawn upward miraculously fuse adjacent slices. Images of at least four cadavers resolve into a single backward autopsy. The pathologist too is a composite. He glimpses Tamagi, Landman, and Michaelson, but the masked face they all share belongs to Andrea.

Taber himself, having refused to perform autopsies on camera, is nowhere to be found.

The backward autopsy concludes with an actor in pale make-up rising from the slab. He blinks his eyes as if seeing the world for the first time. This final scene—judging from the proximity of a bicycle and the exposed wall-studs—must have been filmed in someone's garage.

Acknowledgements

I'm grateful for incisive readings by Geoff Hayden, Jim Wood, Maureen Brady, and John L'Heureux. Many thanks to Charles and Clydette de Groot; Sylvia Whitman and all at Shakespeare and Company; the organizers and judges of the Paris Literary Prize; and Jacques Testard and *The White Review*. Thanks also to Phil Ciampa, Rob Lathan, Bud Smith, Rosemary Smith, Tyler Smith, Gene Willis, and Stefani Willis. And to Brooke Smith, for her love and support, no words are enough.

MMXIII

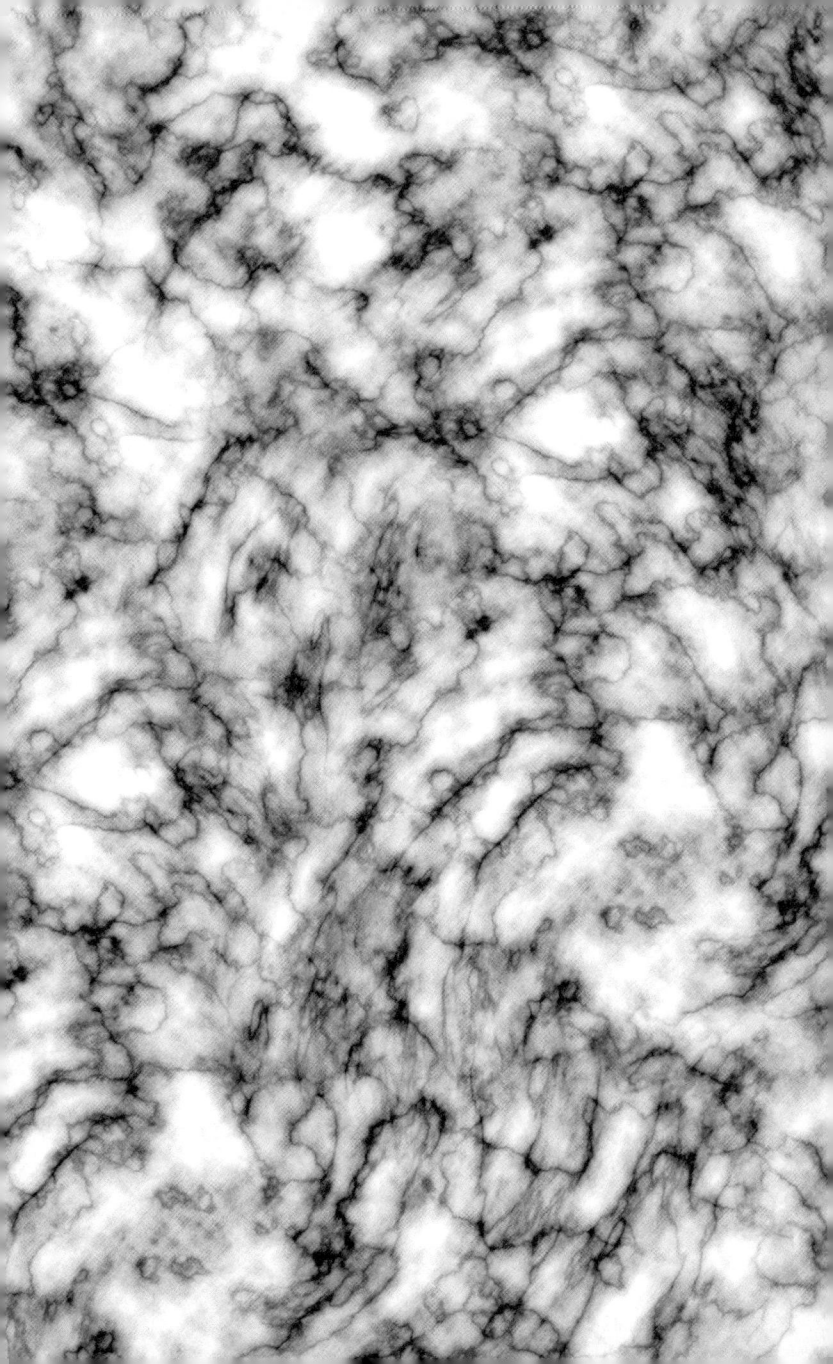

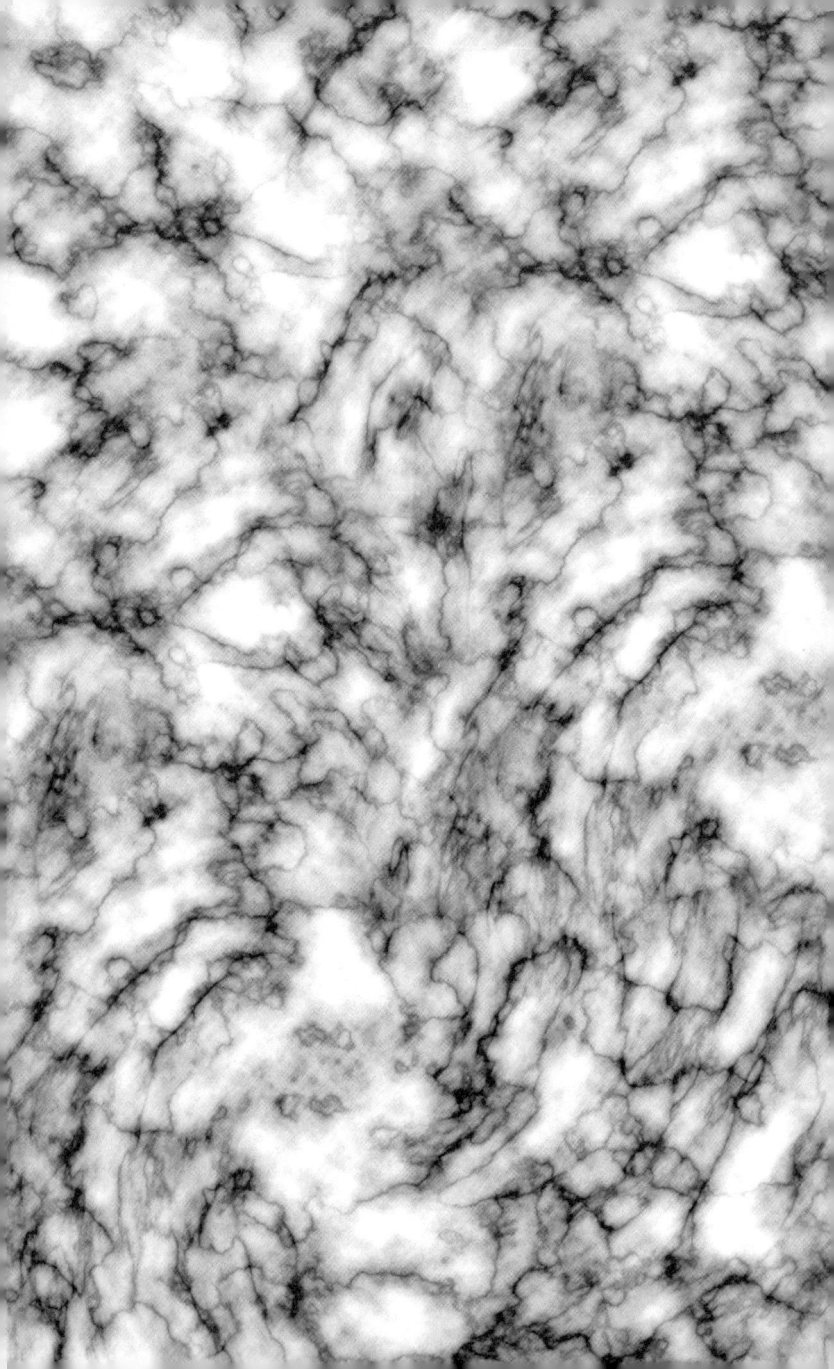